Trackdown

Gregory Payette

8 Flags Publishing, Inc.

Also by Gregory Payette

Visit GregoryPayette.com for the complete catalog:

HENRY WALSH MYSTERIES

Dead at Third

The Last Ride

The Crystal Pelican

The Night the Music Died

Dead Men Don't Smile

Dead in the Creek

Dropped Dead

Dead Luck

A Shot in the Dark

Dead or a Lie

JOE SHELDON SERIES

Play It Cool

Play It Again

Play It Down

U.S. MARSHAL CHARLIE HARLOW

Shake the Trees

Trackdown

Half Moon Rising

Join the email newsletter!

v

Be the first to know about my new releases, subscriber-only sales, and author news and updates. Visit **GregoryPayette.com** to join.

Chapter 1

Charlie could tell by the look on Lindsey's face, she'd had enough of the two young men down the other end of the bar.

Other than the two fools and the music down low on the jukebox, it was quiet at the Coyote Grille. The rough-sawn plank walls gave the long and narrow place the warm feel Charlie liked, on top of it being somewhat dark, other than the dim, canned lights hanging over the bar from the ceiling by cords. The only other light came from the streetlamp outside over the parking lot, shining through the windows at the backs of the two men.

There was a new country song playing that Charlie had never heard before. He didn't like the new stuff very much and preferred *traditional* country: songs by musicians who weren't even around anymore. He always said Johnny Cash made whiskey taste better.

A cool breeze came in through the door that Lindsey, the bartender, liked to leave open a crack. Feeling it at his back had him thinking how fast the summers went by, darkness setting in earlier with each passing day.

The Coyote Grille was up on the second level, with a deck outside the door overlooking the parking lot. It was above a couple of retail establishments down on the ground floor. One was a flower shop and the other some kind of music store that never seemed to be open. Charlie remembered an accountant or some kind of bookkeeper with an office down there, in the back, but never thought to see if he was still there.

Lindsey lived upstairs in the loft apartment over the bar, making it convenient when Charlie didn't feel like driving home. Or when she didn't want to be alone. She could handle herself, kept a 12-gauge behind the bar, but sometimes he worried about her when he wasn't there, especially with a couple of clowns like the two at the end of the bar, who had been drinking all day.

Charlie held his glass of Jack Daniels up in front of him, looking to his right out of the corner of his eye. He nudged his boss, Chief Deputy Frank Carter, as Lindsey told the two young men to finish up their beers, they'd had enough.

Jessie and Dustin didn't appear to like that very much.

Frank gave Charlie a look like he didn't want anything to do with it, sipped from his glass, and stared straight ahead. His voice low, he said, "Let's just hope they finish up and get out of here. I'm not in the mood for dealing with any small-town bullshit right now." He finished what was left in his glass and pushed it forward on the bar.

Charlie was familiar with Dustin and Jessie Redhouse, two brothers who had been in and out of the courthouse Charlie and Frank worked out of. He'd never personally had to deal with either of them, but Charlie knew when they were around, and there was booze involved, there was always a chance there'd be trouble.

He couldn't help but hear every word Dustin and Jessie were saying, their voices louder with each drink.

Dustin was the younger of the two. "She's gotta be out of high school," he said. "Sleeps out there by the fountain on the concrete bench." He laughed. "Got her own pool, can go in and skinny-dip whenever she wants."

Frank had said something, but Charlie's ears were locked on the two brothers, trying to piece together what they might've been talking about. He leaned toward Frank. "You hearin' any of this?"

Frank shook his head. "I told you, I don't want to have to deal with those two idiots. In fact, one more drink and I'm heading home, get my beauty rest."

Frank started to say something else, but Charlie put his hand on Frank's arm. "Shhh." He looked straight ahead toward the shelves of liquor on the back wall but listened with his good ear.

Dustin said, "I heard she puts on a bikini at night, goes in the fountain, picks out all the coins people tossed in. I bet she pulls twenty dollars a day."

Jessie, the older of the two, was almost twice the size of his skinny younger brother. He lifted his mug by the handle and guzzled what was left of his beer. "Twenty's a couple of good meals," he said, laughing. His face went serious, turning to Dustin. "She any good looking at all?"

Lindsey poured Frank another drink and pushed the glass toward him, looking at Charlie like she knew what he was thinking, his eyes focused on the two brothers. She had a worried look on her face and walked down the other end toward the two brothers, using her hands to lean on the bar in front of them. She said, "What's this I hear you two talkin' about?"

Dustin and Jessie both straightened out on their stools and looked up at Lindsey. They shrugged, shaking their heads.

"Nothin'," Jessie said.

"Well, I heard what you were saying, and it didn't sound like nothing. Something about a girl? Living outside?"

Dustin, the younger one, nodded. "She's living at the Fillmore Shopping Center, sleeps outside by the fountain, right there in front of that Mexican place."

Jessie elbowed his brother hard, like he wanted Dustin to keep his mouth shut.

"*What!*" Dustin said, rubbing his arm, looking at Jessie.

"You know who she is?" Lindsey said, peeking over her shoulder at Charlie and Frank, both watching her now.

Jessie and Dustin shook their heads.

Charlie leaned into Frank, his voice low. "I hope these two idiots don't think about driving over there, doing something stupid over at that shopping center. I don't like the idea, all those beers in 'em already, got their minds on a young woman who no doubt's vulnerable."

Frank's phone rang. He picked it up from the bar and looked at the screen, standing up from his stool. He said to Charlie, "I gotta take this one outside." He threw back his drink and turned for the door. "Order us one more, will you?" The door creaked as Frank opened it, then he pushed on the screen door and stepped outside.

The evening air was cool on Charlie's back, the door wide open now. He turned and looked through the screen at the moon shining over the tall pine trees surrounding the parking lot. Frank stood on the far end of the deck, his back to Charlie, leaning on the rail with the phone up to his ear.

Charlie got up and closed the interior door, leaving it open enough to keep the fresh air coming in. As he sat back down on his stool, he heard Lindsey tell the brothers they'd had enough.

She walked over to Charlie, the brothers watching her from behind like they'd never seen a woman's backside before.

Charlie lifted his glass and cleared his throat loud enough for the two to hear. "Let's show a little respect, all right?"

"I can handle myself," Lindsey said, keeping her voice quiet. She picked up Frank's glass. "He stick you with the tab again?"

Charlie smiled, shaking his head. "He's outside on a call." He finished his drink and placed the empty glass in front of him.

Lindsey grabbed the bottle of Jack Daniels from the shelf behind her and filled both Charlie's and Frank's glasses.

Dustin, the younger brother with the big mouth, slapped his hand down on the bar. "Hey, if you're still pouring for them, then why can't we have no more?"

Jessie said, "Come on, Lindsey, give us one more."

Lindsey rolled her eyes and looked at Charlie, acting as if she hadn't heard them.

"Hey!" Jessie yelled. "You hear me?"

Lindsey had a look like she knew she'd already made a mistake giving the brothers one beer too many.

"How about a couple sodas?" she said, picking up a bottle from the shelf, wiping it down with a towel.

"We don't want no goddamn sodas," Dustin said, pushing up his sleeves, showing off the tattoos running up and down each arm.

Charlie glanced toward the door, wondering if Frank would be on his way back inside. He didn't like where things were going, both Redhouse brothers not as bad as some of the others until too much liquor flowed through their blood.

For Charlie, having a drink or three was a way to relax after a hard day's work, knowing the next day would be harder if he had too much. And as much as he liked the Coyote Grille and the pretty proprietor behind the bar, he didn't like the almost weekly occurrence of having to deal with a fool who couldn't handle his liquor.

Charlie had asked her more than once if she'd ever consider selling the place. He'd said to her at one point, "What about hiring a full-time bouncer?" But she couldn't afford to do either, she'd said to Charlie. Not unless a rich man came in and swept her off her feet so she didn't have to work another day in her life.

But the truth was, she could take care of herself with the Mossberg twelve gauge she kept behind the bar and a Smith & Wesson .38 tucked behind the register. Growing up in Weaverville, on the northern edge of Asheville, Lindsey knew most of the people who walked into her bar. That included not only the Redhouse brothers, but their now deceased father, who used to sit on the same end of the bar as his sons.

Charlie didn't know much about their upbringing, other than they'd been raised by their mother after the father had been killed holding up a convenience store out in Marshall, just east of Weaverville.

"Can't we please just have one more?" Jessie said. "We ain't driving." He'd tried to change his tone, like a child begging for a cookie, but Charlie wasn't buying.

Lindsey grabbed the broom and started sweeping behind the bar. "I've learned my lesson with you boys," she said.

Dustin grabbed his empty mug and turned in his stool, raising the mug over his head and tossing it behind him. The glass smashed against the wall on a painting between the two windows and shattered into pieces.

Charlie was on his feet and down the other end of the bar before Dustin had a chance to turn around in his seat, ripping him from the stool by his shirt. He pinned him on the floor without much effort and pressed his knee down onto his chest.

But Jessie was up from his seat and grabbed Charlie from behind, had his arms wrapped around Charlie's neck, trying to wrestle him off his brother.

Charlie held on to Dustin with one hand, had his shirt bunched up in his closed fist, and threw a quick elbow behind him, catching Jessie square in the mouth.

Jessie went crashing into the table behind them and tipped it over as he fell to the floor. He got up on his feet, holding his face with one hand; blood dripping from his mouth through his fingers. He ran for the door and took off outside, leaving his brother behind. The screen door slammed closed behind him.

Lindsey yelled for Charlie to let him go, coming around the bar with the broom still in her hand.

Charlie looked up at her, wondered if she was going to hit him with the handle but eased up his grasp on Dustin's shirt.

Dustin got up, stumbling, nearly tripping over himself trying to get out of there. He brushed past Lindsey, almost knocking her back as he ran for the door after his big brother.

"Goddamnit," Lindsey said, looking down at all the broken glass. She grabbed the tab she'd left for them and turned, holding it up for Charlie as he lifted the table from the floor. She said, "You could've at least waited until they paid their tab."

The door opened, and Frank walked in, looking behind him toward the outside. "What the hell'd you do now?" he said, eyes on Charlie.

Charlie picked his hat off the floor and didn't answer, brushing the dust off the bill. He looked at his hand, feeling something sharp, like he might've had a piece of glass stuck in it. He picked at his finger, removed a tiny shard sticking out from it. Placing his hat back on his head, he gave Frank a nod. "Dustin dropped his mug."

Frank looked down at the hardwoods as Charlie crouched down with a dustpan to help Lindsey sweeping up the broken mug.

She took the dustpan from Charlie and started back to the other side of the bar. "You two go on over and finish up," she said, looking toward the clock behind the bar. "I'm closing early." She walked around the bar with the broom in one hand and the dustpan filled with glass in the other, disappearing through the swinging door and into the back.

Charlie and Frank went over and sat down again, and Frank said, "I don't understand why she keeps letting those boys back in."

Charlie picked up his glass, held it in front of his chin. "She wouldn't have any customers; she kicked out all the ones who caused trouble."

———

Charlie walked a few steps behind Frank across the parking lot, looked up at the full moon coming over the trees. He zipped his jacket and said, "Cold feels like it's coming in early this year. I'm not sure I'm ready for it. Not that I like all that heat this summer much, either."

Frank headed for his car without much else to say but stopped and turned when Charlie said his name.

"I was thinking," Charlie said. "You think one of us should drive by Fillmore Shopping Center?"

Frank appeared to be thinking it over, then looked at his watch. "What are you looking to accomplish? Smartest thing might be, call the local police."

Charlie looked over toward the Suburban he'd been driving. "I've gotta drive down and see Jennie."

"This late?" Frank said.

Charlie nodded. "Was supposed to be there a half hour ago. Something about hiring someone to fix the railing on the front steps."

"You can't fix it yourself?" Frank had a funny look on his face, like he was holding back a grin.

"Well, what I should do is remind her it's not my house anymore. But either way, she said someone'll fall, break their neck by the time I got around to fixing it myself."

Frank opened the driver's-side door of his blue Ford F-150, resting one foot up on the running board. "I have to go by the office, check on a few things. I can swing by the shopping center, if it'll help you sleep tonight."

Charlie thought for a moment. "You know what? I'll go there now. It's on my way out to see Jennie." He started to turn from Frank but stopped. "I just don't like the idea of those Redhouse boys, having a young girl on their minds in there, all those drinks they had inside 'em."

Frank stepped up into his truck, leaned out with his hand on the door's inside handle. "Like I said, probably something for the locals to contend with. But I know sometimes you just can't help yourself." Frank closed the door and started the engine. He drove off without another word, tires crunching on the broken asphalt.

Charlie watched the taillights on Frank's truck disappear beyond the trees and turned for his Suburban. Under his breath, even though Frank was gone, he said, "See you in the morning, boss."

Chapter 2

CHARLIE WALKED ACROSS ONE of the parking lots at the Fillmore Shopping Center, having a hard time remembering the last time he'd been there. It was more run-down at the time with half the stores gone. But it looked like a different place, all new with mostly national chains, like you see in just about any shopping center in Anytown, USA.

The fountain was still there, and he remembered it well, back when he and Jennie used to go a couple times a week for lunch when they were married. But the restaurant they used to order from looked to be gone, replaced with yet another take-out restaurant chain. He had a friend who had been in the restaurant business, but had gotten out with the high rents only the chains could afford. It was why Charlie would drive a little out of his way to get a drink or a sandwich at the Coyote Grille. Other than, of course, to see Lindsey. A good hole-in-the-wall that would stick around for a couple of generations was hard to come by.

He walked over the wood-plank bridge crossing over what looked to be a man-made brook and looked past the empty black tables with open umbrellas. There were a few people eating at a roped-off patio at a place called Four Brothers Burgers, which Charlie thought might've been owned by some Hollywood actor and his siblings, but couldn't remember which.

He walked past a stage with a sign that said LIVE MUSIC EVERY FRIDAY NIGHT THROUGH THE LAST WEEKEND IN SEPTEMBER.

But it was already October.

The sound from the fountain's jets shooting water into the air grew louder as he approached the far end of the outdoor area, the water glistening in the colored lights pointed up toward the dark sky. He liked the peaceful sounds of the fountain, but it still felt artificial, as did everything else around him.

His phone rang, and he removed it from his pocket. When he saw it was Jennie, he knew it wouldn't be good. He should have been there already. "Hey, Jennie," he said, answering.

"Charlie?" she said, her voice raised. "What the hell is wrong with you? I asked you to be here an hour ago. The contractor's on his way now."

"You asked, but I told you I wouldn't be able to get there that soon. I had some work to do."

Although it was late, there were a handful of kids running around, the parents watching but not paying much attention. As much as Charlie despised his father for most of his life, he was glad he took him out to the mountains and taught him the beauty of nature instead of dragging him to a fountain at a shopping center because it was convenient.

Jennie was yapping in Charlie's ear, but he was only half listening, looking for a young woman who may appear to be homeless, whatever that would even look like.

"Did you hear me?" Jennie said.

And all Charlie could do was be honest. "No, not really. You're yelling."

"I'm not yelling," she said. "You said you'd help me with this railing."

"It's just a railing, Jennie. Not that big a deal."

"So you're not coming?"

"Yes, I'm coming. I just had to make a quick stop." He looked at his watch. "Should be there in ten, fifteen minutes." Of course, he knew it would take him at least twenty to get to Hendersonville, if he drove fast enough. "I'm sorry, Jennie. I'm looking for a girl. A young woman."

"I told you already, what you do with your personal life is none of my business anymore."

"Not like that," he said. "I'm at the Fillmore Shopping Center. By the fountain where we used to come eat."

"Oh," she said, but that was it. The line was quiet for a moment.

"I'll see you soon. I'm sorry to keep you waiting." He hung up the phone without giving her a chance to say another word, tucked his phone in his pocket, and sat on the concrete edge of the fountain, tucking his boots in underneath him so he didn't trip one of the kids running by. He looked all around but didn't see a girl who might fit what he had in mind. It was mostly couples, looking like kids themselves, with their young kids.

A man just a few feet away helped a young boy stand on top of the fountain's edge and toss pennies in.

There was no sign of the girl. And no sign of Dustin or Jessie, either.

Charlie looked at the time on his phone and headed for the parking lot, dialing his phone to call Frank as he walked back to his vehicle. "I'm leaving the shopping center right now," he said. "No girl here that I could find."

"You see the brothers?" Frank said.

"No. Nothing."

Frank was quiet on the other end. "I left Chief Brayden a message to call me, let him know about her. I'm not sure there's much any of us'll be able to do." He paused on the other end. "Charlie, I'm sure someone out there appreciates your concern. But you also have to remember the source. We have no way of knowing for sure the story those two clowns were spouting holds any truth."

Charlie pointed his key fob at the Suburban and unlocked the doors, stepping up inside. "I thought about that," he said. "Or maybe she's gone home."

———

Charlie made it down to Jennie's house—*his* house, before they divorced—in just under twenty minutes, on top of the ten he'd spent looking around the shopping center before he left.

He turned in the driveway but had to back out when a truck parked behind Jennie's car had the reverse lights on. Charlie waited in the street in front of the house, gave the man in the truck a nod as he drove past him, then pulled back into the driveway.

Jennie was in the doorway watching Charlie, and he could see it in her face. *She's in one of her moods,* he thought. He walked over the brick walkway toward the front door.

"You're unbelievable," she said, looking out through the screen. "You promised me you'd be here to meet the contractor."

Charlie shook his head. "I told you I could be here, just not as soon as you wanted me to be." Charlie looked back at the red lights on the rear of the contractor's truck as it disappeared down the road. "Why's he coming out so late? When it's dark out?"

Jennie pushed open the door and held it open. "I assume he's on the job all day." She just about let it close on him and turned from the door as he reached for the handle.

Charlie stepped inside. "It's just a railing," he said. "Can't imagine there's much involved in fixing it." He looked around the living room just inside to his left. The furniture was different. He could smell it: brand-new furniture and whatever chemicals they spray on them. "What'd you do with my old couch?"

"Got rid of it."

"*Got rid of it?*" he said. "It was brand new."

Jennie laughed, stepping out from the kitchen with a glass of red wine in one hand, a cut carrot in her other. She took a bite of the carrot, using it to point into the living room area with the new furniture. "We've had that couch since we first got married, Charlie. It was time for it to go. And besides, it didn't match the new paint."

Charlie looked at the walls and hadn't even noticed the new off-white color, when he first walked in. "I would've taken it, if you'd told me you were getting rid of it."

"And do *what* with it?" she said. "I don't think it'd even fit in that trailer you're living in now."

"It's a Winnebago," he said.

Jennie walked back into the kitchen and opened the refrigerator, her back to Charlie. "You want a beer?"

He said, "Does this mean you're not mad?"

She took out a bottle of Yuengling and opened the top, handing it to him. She threw the cap in the garbage under the sink and poured more wine into her glass. "I just wish you'd keep your word," she said. "That's all."

Charlie didn't even bother trying to explain. He'd made it clear he couldn't be there when she wanted him to. It was a losing battle with Jennie, no matter what. It was different when they were first married, happy for those first bunch of years. But then it just turned into, no matter what he said, him being the one who was wrong. Always. Even though they were divorced, it hadn't changed much at all. If he said something was black, she'd say it was white.

"You're the one who keeps telling me not to let anyone in here I don't know, without you being around. What was I supposed to tell that man? You'll have to come back, my ex-husband's not here?"

Charlie sipped his beer. "I told you on the phone, I went by the Fillmore Shopping Center to check on a girl—a young woman—supposedly living there, outside. I don't know what the story is. But she wasn't there, so maybe she's not anymore."

"Isn't that something for the police to deal with?"

Charlie nodded. "It is, normally. But I was at the Coyote Grille and—"

"The Coyote Grille?" Jennie huffed. "You said you were working late, not going to your girlfriend's bar."

Charlie cracked a small smile. He couldn't help but like when Jennie got jealous, even though he never wanted Jennie to find out about Lindsey in the first place.

"I met Frank. But if you'd let me finish..."

Jennie looked back at him, sipping her wine.

He said, "There are these two brothers who were there. Been in and out of trouble since they were kids. And when they started talking about this young woman they'd heard had been sleeping at the shopping center by the fountain, I just thought..."

Jennie said, "You think they'd go over there? Cause trouble?"

"Wouldn't put it past either of them," Charlie said. "You know, if something were to happen to her and I didn't at least make some kind of effort to make sure she was all right…"

Jennie held her wineglass up in front of her mouth, a look on her face like she was trying to cover up a smile.

"Did I say something funny?" Charlie said, staring back at her.

"No, not at all. I'm sorry."

"Then what's that smirk on your face?"

She looked toward the floor, then raised her gaze to Charlie. "You're a good guy, Charlie Harlow."

He said, "If you think so highly of me, why'd we divorce?"

Jennie rolled her eyes. "Can't I just say something nice about you without having to go down this road every time?" She turned and started back into the kitchen.

Charlie looked her over from behind. "You still look the way you did when we were married, you know."

"You mean, from behind?" She turned and looked back over her shoulder, down at herself.

Charlie laughed.

Jennie picked up a yellow sheet of paper off the counter. "Here's the quote for the work on the steps."

Charlie reached out and took it from her, looking it over with his eyes open wide. "Is he serious? This much? To fix a railing?"

She shook her head. "I told you already, if you'd only listen. It's not just the railing. He has to re-cement the steps... or whatever you call it."

Charlie wasn't sure. Re-cement sounded about right. He'd worked construction when he was younger, before he decided to join the Marshals Service, but it was never really his thing.

"So what are you going to do about the girl?" she said. "Is she okay?"

Charlie raised his eyes from the paper and put it back down on the counter. He thought for a moment, then shrugged. "Frank already left a message with Asheville PD. Chief Brayden. Hopefully, they won't just brush it off."

Chapter 3

It was early morning when Charlie poured himself a coffee and stepped out the door of his Winnebago, parked on the edge of the Swannanoa River. Steam rose from his cup in the cold air as Charlie took a sip, watching the sun creeping up in the distance through the trees. The property was owned by a friend of Charlie's who'd said he could stay there as long as he liked. He told Charlie he planned to build a house there one day but wasn't sure he'd ever get to it.

Charlie had gotten the 1983 Winnebago from the auction, but at the time had no idea it would one day become his home. It was only after his divorce from Jennie was final, he decided he didn't need a house. And he couldn't see living in one of those new apartments with all those people crammed together in one building.

He sat down on a picnic table with his coffee, staring out at the river. A flock of birds flew high in formation, and Charlie thought, with the early chill, they were heading south. He kept his eyes on the birds until they disappeared beyond the trees. He never minded the cold and remembered Jennie saying one day they should retire to Florida.

Not his thing, he told her.

He sat, quiet, enjoying the fresh air and quiet all around him. He hadn't been able to get the girl, sleeping at the shopping center, off his mind, and started to wonder if he'd looked hard enough. He should've gone back after he left Jennie's.

What if the brothers showed up when she was there, after the crowd had gone?

———

The Fillmore Shopping Center was empty and quiet, other than the sound of a single-engine plane flying high over Charlie's head.

He walked toward the fountain and over the wooden footbridge, from the parking lot, the sounds of the fountain growing louder as it covered over the quiet. The sun was up high enough now, he could see the water from the fountain sparkle in the morning sun's rays. He sipped the coffee he'd picked up on the drive out—as if he hadn't had enough caffeine already—and looked back and forth at the closed shops and restaurants on either side of where he walked. Everything looked to be at least a couple of hours from opening.

He didn't see any sign of the girl. At least not until he stepped closer to the fountain and looked across, through the jets of water, and saw someone lying flat on a bench, covered with a blanket. He walked closer and saw long, dark hair coming out from under it, hanging down.

He waited, watching for movement before he went around to the other side of the fountain. He didn't want to startle her, although he could only assume it was the girl he'd gone there looking for.

As he stepped closer, he wasn't exactly sure what he would say or how she would react to a stranger walking up to her, asleep on a bench in a shopping center well before seven in the morning.

Even with the bright sun coming out of the blue sky, the air had a pretty good chill to it. With October right around the corner, he couldn't imagine how she could continue sleeping outside.

Charlie stood over her and removed his sunglasses, squinting as he reached down and tapped her on the shoulder. "Hey, are you okay?"

The girl's eyes sprang open, and she jumped into a seated position, her feet up on the bench. She tucked her legs close to her chest with her arms wrapped around her knees, holding them against her. "Who the hell are you?" she said, looking up at him.

Charlie had his badge ready in his hand. "Deputy U.S. Marshal Charlie Harlow. I'm here to... I just want to make sure you're all right. I'm not going to hurt you."

She didn't respond at first, staring back at him like she'd just come out of a deep sleep, looking around the fountain as if she was getting ready to run.

Charlie was surprised how young she looked. Younger than he'd expected. She really was just a kid. "Like I said, I'm just checking to make sure you're okay." He looked past her at the wooded area between where they stood and the parking lot on the other side, fifty yards away. "I'm just not sure this is a safe place for a young lady to be sleeping out here, all alone."

She swallowed, nodding. "I'm... I'm fine."

Charlie said, "What's your name?"

"Are you really a marshal?"

He nodded.

"Do you stop terrorists from hijacking planes?"

Charlie smiled. He'd heard that one at least a few dozen times before. "That's the US Air Marshals." He pointed to the emblem on the chest of his jacket. "U.S. Marshals Service. I don't even like to fly."

"So, like the police?"

"No, not really."

"Not really?"

He paused, smiling again at the young girl's inquisitive nature. She seemed confident enough, less worried about living outside on a bench than most people might be. "You going to tell me your name?"

"Haley."

"You have a last name, Haley?"

"Am I in trouble?"

He shook his head. "Not at all, Haley. I told you already, I was just checking up on you."

She squinted her eyes, reached into a plastic GAP bag under the bench and took out a pair of sunglasses. The bag looked to be stuffed with clothes. "Haley Moore," she said, looking up at Charlie. She put her feet down on the concrete and folded up the blanket.

Charlie lifted his sunglasses from his pocket and slipped them over his eyes. He looked around and through the fountain's jets, seeing someone walking into one of the shops, assuming it was a person who worked there, opening up for the day. "Listen, so how long've you been sleeping out here like this?"

She shrugged. "I don't know. Three weeks, I guess?"

"Three weeks? You've been living out here like this for three weeks? That's a long time, isn't it? And nobody's bothered you?"

She shrugged again. "People are nice around here, for the most part." She held up the folded blanket. "Some lady came by and gave me this a few nights ago, when the temperature dropped."

"You don't have anywhere else you can stay? Relatives? Parents? Something happen to them?"

She looked down toward the ground. "Just my dad. But we don't get along."

"No?" Charlie almost wanted to tell her he knew first-hand what she meant but didn't go into it. He waited, thinking maybe she'd offer more. "So you're dad's all right with you out here all by yourself, sleeping on a bench?"

She didn't respond, looking straight ahead now toward the fountain's water spraying high into the air.

And Charlie didn't want to push, make her say anything more than she was comfortable saying. He noticed a bottle of ketchup under the bench and wondered if that might've been her dinner. "You want something to eat?"

She looked at him, shaking her head. "No, I'm good."

"You're good?" he said. "It doesn't look like you're good." He grinned. "Just being honest with you, Haley."

She let out a crooked smile, bouncing her heel off the concrete.

"How about I go get you some food, huh? Bring it back so you have something to eat for breakfast?"

A slight breeze came across the area, blowing Haley's hair down over her sunglasses. She pushed it back and used her sunglasses to keep it in place on top of her head. With her eyes squinted, she looked up at Charlie. "I'm okay."

He wasn't buying it. "I'm sure you are. But you need to eat. I'm just offering to grab you something. We don't have to make a big deal about it, all right?"

She slipped her sunglasses back down over her eyes.

"You eat eggs? Bagels?"

With a shrug, she nodded again. "Sure."

"I bet a hot coffee would do you all right, too, huh?"

She smiled this time. "Thanks."

"Will you be right here when I get back?"

"I don't have anywhere else to go just yet."

Charlie's phone rang in his pocket as he walked out from Benny's Bagel Shop on the other side of the shopping center, a bag with two bagel sandwiches in one hand and a tray with a coffee and a clear plastic bottle of orange juice in the other. He walked across the street to where he'd parked the Suburban and put the bag on the hood, but was too late by the time he'd taken his phone out to answer.

But as soon as he saw it was Kim—Deputy U.S. Marshal Kim Riggins—he tapped the screen and returned her call without waiting to see if she'd left a message. "You looking for me?" he said as soon as she answered.

"Frank is. He asked me to call, see if you were coming to the office."

Charlie unlocked the driver's-side door and opened it, placing the cardboard tray on top of the center console. "Why wouldn't I be coming in?" He stepped around the door and grabbed the bag off the hood.

"I'm not exactly sure. He's in one of his moods, forgets I'm not his secretary. Sounds like he's got something for you: failure to appear, down in Hendersonville. I think he may've hoped you were still down at your house."

"Well, it's not my house anymore. And I wouldn't be down there." He stepped into the Suburban and slid the key into the ignition. "I'm ten minutes from the office. You think he wants me to go down there?"

Kim sighed into the phone. "You're asking questions you know I can't answer. Between the two of you..."

Charlie laughed. "Tell him I'll give him a call as soon as I'm done."

"Done with *what*? I have to tell him something."

"Uh, I'm at the Fillmore Shopping Center. Just gotta take care of something."

"This have something to do with the young woman sleeping over there, on the bench?"

"Frank told you? I'm not even sure I'd call her a young woman. She's a kid. A girl."

Charlie had already jumped back on 26 and took the first exit, not even a quarter mile away, onto Fillmore Parkway. He drove into the shopping center lot closest to the fountain, parking the Suburban in a space to the left of the footbridge.

"You know how old she is?" Kim said.

"I don't. I'd be surprised she's even eighteen, nineteen maybe."

"Well, that's not a little girl, Charlie."

He stepped out and tucked the bag with the two sandwiches under his arm, held the phone with his shoulder, carried the tray in one hand, and grabbed his phone with the other.

Kim said, "Did you find her?"

"Yeah, I actually talked to her. She didn't say much, but I'm bringing her something to eat right now." He walked over the bridge and saw a man with a long pole down across the courtyard, standing on the edge of the fountain. The water jets were turned off, and the man appeared to be doing some work to it or maybe just cleaning it out.

Charlie was too far away to be sure, but when he looked through the jets of water, he didn't see Haley on the other side. "Kim, let me call you back, all right?"

"What do you want me to tell Frank?" she said.

"I don't know. Give me a few minutes. I'll call you right back." He hung up without another word, walked around the fountain to the empty bench. He looked around, wondering where she could've gone and why she didn't wait for him, like she said she would.

He went back around to the other side where the man had a long pole with a net on the other end, skimming leaves and debris from the top of the fountain's pool. Charlie approached him. "Morning."

The man turned and gave him a nod. "Good morning."

Charlie said, "You happen to see a girl, a young lady, over there on that bench? Was here maybe about fifteen minutes ago?"

The man nodded. "Of course. She's here all the time." He looked Charlie over. "Who are *you*?"

Charlie held up the white bag, holding the tray in his other hand. "Just brought her some breakfast." He didn't pull his badge. He didn't think he needed to, not when he wasn't technically acting under any kind of official business. "Any chance you know where she might've gone?"

The man shook his head, removed the skimmer from the water and emptied whatever was inside it with his hands, into a bucket next to him. "I don't usually see her around during the day. She's here early in the morning but usually disappears once people start showing up. At least until later in the evening."

Charlie put the bag and tray on top of the fountain's edge. "If you see her, would you mind making sure she gets this?"

The man looked down at the food and drinks, nodding. "Sure thing."

"Thank you," Charlie said. He started to walk away and stopped, turning back to the man. "She don't show up, go ahead and help yourself. Hate to see it all go to waste."

Chapter 4

CHARLIE WALKED INTO THE U.S. Marshals Service office on the second floor of the Buncombe County Courthouse, tried to avoid making eye contact with Frank sitting in his office behind the glass, until he had a chance to get to his desk.

But Frank called out to him.

Charlie headed over, stood in the doorway with a take-out cup of coffee in his hand. "Morning," he said, taking a sip.

Frank gestured with his hand for Charlie to close the door. "Have a seat." He opened a folder on his desk, slipping his reading glasses over his eyes, looking it over. He folded it, sliding the folder across the desk toward Charlie.

Charlie put his cup down on Frank's desk, grabbed the folder and opened it on his lap. He looked at the first page, a photo attached to the left side with a paperclip.

"This him? James Keegan? The one down in Hendersonville?"

"Federal warrant for his arrest. Supervised-release violation, after being charged with passing counterfeit currency."

"James Keegan?" Charlie said, flipping through the papers.

"Shouldn't be much to it, I wouldn't think. Investigation took ten minutes, traced him down at his sister's house, not far from your house."

Charlie looked up from the folder. "You always say it like you want to hear me say it's not my house anymore. You get a kick out of it?"

Frank grinned, shaking his head. "Can you handle it alone?"

Charlie stood up from the chair and turned for the door.

"Hang on a moment," Frank said. "Kim said you were over at the shopping center again?"

Charlie leaned against the edge of the doorway. "She was there this time. Spoke to her for a few minutes. Seems to have a decent head on her shoulders, but didn't tell me much about why she's living out on the streets. Went and got her some breakfast, brought it back, and she was gone."

"Gone?" Frank said, removing his glasses from his face.

Charlie shrugged. "Guess she wasn't that hungry."

Frank leaned back in his big leather chair, picked up a pen and twisted it between both hands. "Charlie, you know there are approximately four million kids living on the streets at any given time in this great country of ours? If that doesn't say we have a problem, I don't know what does. We have units involved, Charlie. But there's only so much we can do."

Charlie nodded, a half-crooked grin on his face. "I'm not trying to solve any big world issues, Frank. Just making sure this girl's safe, got something to eat."

"I admire that," Frank said, nodding toward the folder in Charlie's hand. "But we've got work to do." He had a small piece of paper torn from a pad, holding it out for Charlie. "Here, give this woman a call. She runs a shelter downtown, see if maybe she can help."

Charlie sipped his coffee. "You talk to Chief Brayden?"

Frank nodded. "He gave me the number."

Charlie looked at the slip of paper. "That's all he could do, huh?" He turned, leaving Frank's office. "I'll call you when I'm done in Hendersonville."

Before heading south on 26 off of 240, Charlie took the exit for Fillmore Parkway and drove into the shopping center. He parked in the same space he had earlier, walked over the footbridge and across the courtyard between the stores and restaurants, now open and buzzing with a crowd outside in what had turned out to be a warm and sunny day, compared to the chill in the air when he first got up.

He walked to the fountain, jets spraying again, the man who was there cleaning earlier nowhere in sight. He wasn't sure he'd find Haley there, either, but took a chance and walked around looking at the tables.

Sure enough, he saw her sitting at a table under an umbrella, shaded from the morning sun. She was reading a paperback book, something Charlie thought you didn't see anymore, the way they spent most waking moments staring at a device. She was turned from the table, slouched down with her feet up on the chair in front of her.

"Haley?" he said, walking up to her table.

She seemed surprised, almost spooked, looking up at Charlie for a second before she smiled. "Oh, hello." She stuck a piece of paper in between the pages she was reading and closed the book.

Charlie glanced at the cover, saw it was some kind of romance novel, by the looks of it. "What're you reading?"

Haley took a look at the cover herself, as if she couldn't remember the title, and held it up to Charlie to show him.

"Marie Force?" he said. "Never heard of her."

"You don't look the type to read romance."

He grinned. "You'd be surprised."

She smiled back and sat up straight in the chair. "Thanks for the breakfast," she said.

"I thought maybe the man I asked to give it to you would've eaten it before you got back."

"Steve?" She shook her head. "He wouldn't do that. He's always nice to me. Sometimes he brings me things to eat."

Charlie glanced over his shoulder at the fountain. "Listen," he said, "the reason I came out here this morning—and how I knew you were here—was I'd overheard a conversation between these two brothers I know a little something about... talking about a young lady sleeping by the fountain out here. Now, they're not the brightest boys you'll ever meet, and they're not always clear on what's right or wrong." He looked down at Haley. "You know what I'm trying to say?"

She held her gaze on him for a moment, finally nodding, like it clicked inside her head. "You said they were brothers?"

Charlie nodded. "You know them?"

She shook her head. "I'm always looking out, wondering who might be looking at me funny, if there's anyone I should be worried about. And there were a couple of older boys here last night. To be honest, kind of had me creeped out a little, the way they were looking at me."

Charlie leaned with his hands on the back of the chair. "What'd they look like?"

She shrugged. "One was tall. Had long hair, a little muscle on him but not much. The other one, they looked alike, but I'd say the other was younger. Skinny and shorter. Skin's kind of dark on both of 'em."

"They say anything to you?"

Haley shook her head. "No. I took off before they could notice. I could tell, by how loud they were, the things they were saying, I'd say they'd been drinking. But I usually know when to get out of there."

Charlie looked around at the people at the other tables, some with kids who appeared to be restless, wanting to run around. Others sat alone, eating or drinking. He looked back at Haley, "You probably already know this, but it's just not safe for you to be out here alone. Not at night. I don't mean to scare you; you seem to have a good enough head on your shoulders, but, just using those two brothers as an example, there are people who aren't playing with a full deck you need to be careful of."

Haley had her hands folded between her legs, her gaze on the table. She didn't respond.

Charlie held out the paper Frank had given him with the number of the women's shelter on it. "I have this number, a woman you can call who runs a shelter for young women like yourself, if—"

"I'm not going to any shelter," she snapped, her eyes almost angry, staring back at Charlie. "I told you already, I'm fine. I can handle myself."

Charlie rubbed the back of his neck, trying to stretch the kink he had from another sleepless night in the Winnebago. "You can't stay here forever." He held up the piece of paper. "At least you can talk to someone who might know about this stuff, what you're going through. I'll admit, it's not my expertise. So if this woman on this paper can at least somehow help you—"

"I'm not going to a goddamn shelter," she said, standing from the table. She tucked her book in her plastic GAP bag stuffed full with the blanket sticking out the top. "I gotta go." She started to walk away and Charlie followed.

"Listen," he said, pulling out his wallet. He took out one of his cards, but she kept walking away from him.

"Haley, hold up. I just want you to take this."

She stopped, turning toward him with tears in her eyes.

"I'm not trying to bother you," he said. "But I'd like you to take this. It'll make me feel better. All right?" He held out the card with his cell phone number written on it. "That's my cell, the one written in pen. You ever get in trouble or someone you think might be bothering you..."

She took the card, looked it over, and tucked it in her back pocket. "Okay. Thanks." She gave him a small grin and walked away.

———

Charlie was on 26 passing a tractor trailer, doing about eighty miles an hour and was halfway to Hendersonville when he picked up the phone and dialed Deputy Kim Riggins.

She picked it up on the first ring. "Are you already looking for help?"

Charlie laughed, leaning with his eyes on the side-view mirror on the passenger side, shifting back over to the right lane once he was past the tractor trailer. "Could you do me a small favor?"

"I guess it depends," Kim said, neither one making the conversation easy on the other.

"Would you mind seeing if there's anything you can dig up about Jessie and Dillon Redhouse? I don't mean what's in their file, but maybe see if there's anything else we should know?"

Kim paused on the other end. "Does this have to do with that girl at the shopping center? Frank said you might be calling me about it, said if you want to check up on the girl on your own time, he's fine with it, but the U.S. Marshals Service can't be involved. We just don't have the resources. He did speak with Chief Brayden. But it didn't sound like there was much he could do."

"Yeah, he gave Frank a number for a homeless shelter. Great work, Chief."

Kim said, "Did you give her the number?"

Charlie glanced at the speedometer, the Suburban moving at a good enough clip, he was ahead of schedule. "She wants nothing to do with going to a shelter. I can't say I blame her."

"So what are you asking me to do?" Kim said.

Charlie stared straight ahead at the highway, thinking. "I couldn't even come up with a recent address for them. I believe they're still up in Weaverville, but the last address on file's no good. Landlord said they'd moved out two months ago."

Kim paused on the other end. "I'll see what I can do." Quiet for a moment, she said, "Are you going to tell me what the goal is, Charlie? The brothers haven't done anything wrong, have they?"

"Not yet," he said. "But she thinks she saw them at the shopping center after apparently driving around liquored up, after they left Coyote Grille. I should've taken their keys, or had them followed."

"What about the girl?" Kim said. "You have her name? I mean, if I'm already going to be looking into it..."

Charlie took the exit for 64, grabbed the paper from the folder with James Craig's sister's address. "Her name's Haley Moore."

Kim spelled it out, "M-O-O-R-E?"

Charlie thought for a second. "I'd say that's about right."

Chapter 5

Charlie merged onto Chimney Rock Road and slowed when he saw the sign for Half-Moon Trail. He turned into the parking lot of the Ballantyne Apartments, and parked the Suburban along the tall fence surrounding the pool with nobody in or around it. He looked at the paper next to him on the seat with Alyssa Craig's apartment number, made sure he was at the right place and folded it up, sticking it in his pocket.

He walked up the open-air stairs of the garden-style apartment building, stepped off onto the second floor, and walked down the hall to apartment 209, the last apartment on the left. He stood outside the door for a moment before he knocked, looking both ways along the hall to identify all paths toward an escape, hoping he wouldn't have to worry about having to chase. He remembered Frank had promised it would be easy.

But he knew it never was.

Charlie had his badge ready and knocked on the door. He turned his right ear to the door, listening for whatever he might be able to hear on the other side.

Barely a half a minute had gone by when the locks clicked, the door opened, and a woman with her hair up, wearing dark-rimmed glasses, stood in the doorway. She had a studious look to her, like a librarian or a teacher, appearing younger than he'd expected. The file had her at thirty-six. She certainly didn't look the type to be hiding a fugitive.

Although Charlie knew how these things worked. Family's family.

"Alyssa Keegan?" he said, lifting his badge and tucking it back in his pocket before she had a chance to look it over. "I'm Deputy U.S. Marshal Charlie Harlow." He held up the warrant. "I'm here for your brother, Mr. James Keegan."

She looked past Charlie, out into the hall, shaking her head. "I'm sorry, but he isn't here. I haven't seen James since before the summer."

Charlie cleared his throat. "Ma'am, we have reports of him being seen coming and going from this apartment. He looked at the number on the wall to the right of the open door. "This looks to be apartment two-oh-nine. And you're his sister, so..."

"I don't know where he is. That's the truth. I'm sorry you've heard otherwise. But I haven't spoken to James in a long time."

Charlie tried to look into the apartment, but she kept her hand on the knob, had the door almost closed behind her.

He said, "You mind I come in?"

She looked at the warrant in his hand and said, "I'm sorry," then closed the door.

Charlie had a good feeling James Keegan was somewhere in that apartment. He knocked on the door and waited, but Alyssa didn't answer the door. Charlie stepped toward the railing overlooking a wooded area and what appeared to be a walking trail cut between the trees. He leaned over and looked to his left at the second-floor balcony. It belonged to Alyssa Keegan's apartment. He heard a glass door slide open, and he backed out of view, poking his head out from behind the wall just enough to see who was about to step outside.

And sure enough, a man in jeans and a T-shirt walked out onto the balcony and started to climb over the railing. He stood on the other side or it, on the very edge of the balcony, grasping the railing behind him, looking down toward the ground, not more than twelve feet below. He hadn't noticed Charlie watching him.

Charlie held his Glock and hung out over the railing he stood behind. He yelled, "James Keegan! Hold it right there."

James looked at Charlie without a word or a second more of hesitation and dropped from the balcony. He hit the ground below with both feet and tumbled over, rolling down a grassy hill before getting back up to his feet and into the wooded area at the back of the building.

"Shit," Charlie said, tucking his Glock back in the holster. He ran for the stairs, skipped every other step and was down on the ground floor, turning down a hall past apartment doors and out the rear of the building, looking into the wooded area.

James Keegan was already far ahead down the path.

"Stop! Police!" Charlie yelled, running onto the same path and through the woods after him, seeing him through the trees heading toward what looked like a church.

James Keegan looked back at him, running faster than Charlie had expected and out of the wooded area, moving across a parking lot and past the church.

Charlie was catching up but still far behind. He lost sight of Keegan around the church, running to the right side of it, hoping to somehow cut him off.

But Keegan was already standing on the side of Route 64, car horns blasting as he stood on the edge of the road, starting to run across. He looked back at Charlie and bolted for the other side. Tires screeched, drivers slamming on their brakes to avoid hitting him.

By the time Charlie made it to the road, Keegan was already running across a shopping center parking lot, with a Home Depot and Texas Roadhouse restaurant.

Charlie dotted across the traffic with his Glock out and yelled for James Keegan to stop.

But Keegan didn't listen right then, not until he stopped and approached an older gentleman stepping out from a white Toyota pickup truck.

Charlie was getting close when he saw Keegan throw the old man to the ground, jump in the driver's seat, and slam the door closed. Charlie raised the Glock, his finger on the trigger as the truck took off, James Keegan behind the wheel.

The Toyota pickup was up on two wheels, tires squealing as Keegan jumped the curb and bounced onto Chimney Rock Road. He cut off an oncoming car and was gone before Charlie could do anything about it.

He watched the truck turn onto Route 26 heading north before it disappeared out of view along the other side of the shopping center.

Breathing heavy and trying to catch his breath, Charlie hurried over to the old man and helped him to his feet. "You all right?"

The old man nodded, brushing off his sleeves, his eyes on the Glock in Charlie's hand. "You a cop?"

Charlie showed the man his badge. "Deputy U.S . Marshal."

The man's eyebrows raised. "No kidding?"

Charlie tucked his gun in the holster and took out his phone, doing his best to control his heavy breathing without much luck. His heart was pounding so hard he could feel it in his ears. He dialed Frank.

"You got him?" Frank said, first words from his mouth when he answered.

Charlie shook his head, looking out toward Chimney Rock Road. "He took off in a stolen vehicle. You don't mind calling it into Hendersonville PD, maybe Highway Patrol?" He took the phone away from his ear and asked the man for his registration number.

"W-V-A-One-Nine-Seven," the man said.

"Frank, got the plate: North Carolina registration William-Virginia-Adam-One-Nine-Seven. White Toyota pickup, last seen heading north on Twenty-Six from Chimney Rock Road."

"I thought you said it would be easy," Frank said, giving it to Charlie as he always did.

"Uh, actually you're the one who said it would be easy, Frank. Man jumped off a second-story balcony, and the sister closed the door in my face."

Frank was quiet for a moment on the other end. "I should've known better, let you go down there alone. I hope your mind was clear enough, worrying about—"

"Frank, you mind just calling Hendersonville PD, before he gets any farther away?"

"Why didn't you just go after him?" Frank said.

"I just told you he stole a man's truck. We were on foot."

"Oh," Frank said. "Let me make the call. Does the man need assistance? Paramedics?"

"I'll take care of him." Charlie hung up and told the man he'd give him a ride but needed to file a stolen vehicle report.

"I'll call my wife," he said. "I got a good look at the son of a bitch, if that'll help."

Charlie said, "I'll see to it you get your truck back, sir."

<hr>

Charlie was back outside the apartment and walked past his Suburban, went straight up the stairs back to apartment 209. He knocked on the door, felt around the handcuffs on his belt, and waited, knowing there was a good chance she was gone. He knocked, turned his ear to the door. "Alyssa Keegan, this is Deputy U.S. Marshal Charlie Harlow. You have ten seconds to open this door, or I'm going to have to open it from the outside." He knocked again, this time pounding it with his fist. "Miss Keegan?"

A gunshot was fired from somewhere out in front of the building. It was followed by another.

Charlie ran for the stairs, looking out into the parking lot toward a blue sedan, which appeared to be a Toyota Camry, driving away from where he'd parked. He made it out to the lot and had a hard time being sure, but it looked like his Suburban was leaning quite a bit toward one side.

The Toyota skidded out from the apartment's entrance and onto Half-Moon Trail. Charlie was sure it was Alyssa Keegan taking off. He hurried to the Suburban and looked down at the front tire, and then at the rear. The rims were just resting on the pavement, both tires flat and completely out of air. He picked up the casing from the gun that was fired, shaking his head as he looked out toward the street.

Chapter 6

It was dark by the time Charlie got his tires replaced. Frank and Kim had driven down to Hendersonville together to meet him. There were half a dozen officers from the Hendersonville Police Department standing around, all assuming James Keegan and his sister, Alyssa, were both long gone. Even with roadblocks set up on back roads and major highways, they were left empty-handed.

The white Toyota pickup James had stolen was recovered, spotted behind Hendersonville Middle School, keys still in the ignition. No sighting of the blue Toyota Camry, however, although the registration was confirmed and belonged to Alyssa.

"What do you want to do now?" Charlie said to Frank, checking his phone to see if there had been any updates.

Frank turned, looking at the apartment. "Chief Holden said he'll have his officers out there throughout the night, but I'd be surprised they're still in the area at this point. Wouldn't you?"

Charlie nodded. "Sorry about this, Frank. I should've—"

"Come on, Charlie. You know better than to apologize for something like this. I'm just surprised you didn't pull your gun, try and take a shot when he was driving away. Good news is you seem to be understanding shoot first, ask questions later doesn't sit right with the Justice Department."

"Well, to be honest, Frank, if I thought I had a shot, I would've taken it. The old man was getting up off the ground, otherwise I'd have at least taken out the tires."

"Or you'd have Keegan in the morgue," Frank said. "And you know that's the last thing you need."

Charlie took off his hat—the U.S. Marshal baseball-style cap he usually wore—scratching his head and fixing his hair before placing it back on his head. "I rarely shoot to kill," he said.

"That's news to me," Frank said, turning from Charlie, heading toward the Hendersonville Police officers standing near the edge of the parking lot.

Charlie's phone rang. He looked at the screen and didn't recognize the 828 area code. He answered the call and put the phone up to his ear. "Deputy Harlow."

"Deputy?" The voice belonged to a young girl, quiet, like she was in a whisper. The traffic going by on the street made it hard for him to hear, she was being so quiet.

"Yes?" Charlie said, looking at Kim watching him. He had a feeling who it was.

"This is Haley. Haley Moore. From the—"

"Haley, yeah. Hi. Is everything all right?"

Her voice was still hushed and almost muffled, like her lips were too close to the phone. "I... I don't know. I'm behind a dumpster at the shopping center."

"Behind a dumpster?" He started toward the Suburban. "What are you... Are you in trouble?"

"There were two men here, watching me. And when I got up and moved, I started toward the parking lot. They followed me."

"Was it the two brothers you said you saw last night?"

"I don't know. I'm not sure."

Charlie looked at his watch. It was nearly eleven o'clock. "They still there now?"

"I don't know. I didn't know what to do, so I ran and hid. I was just thinking about what you told me, and... what if they're looking for me?" Her voice shook in her whisper.

"Okay, Haley. Listen to me. I'm going to call someone right now, get the police over there to help you. I'll be there as soon as I can. Can you hang tight for a few minutes?"

She was quiet, a noise coming through the phone like she'd started to cry. "I'm scared."

Charlie's throat was dry. He lifted the phone away from his mouth and said to Kim, "Get someone from the Asheville Police on the phone right away—anyone you can call direct—tell them there's a young woman hiding behind a dumpster at the Fillmore Shopping Center." Charlie moved the phone back toward his mouth. "Haley, where exactly are you? Which dumpster? Is there a store, or—"

"Around the back of the building, behind..." She paused. "I think I'm behind Cabo's, the Mexican place."

"Okay, yeah, listen. Haley, don't worry. Is there anyone else around you? Do you see anyone else who can help you?"

The line was quiet. "Haley?" Charlie's heart raced. He looked at Kim, already on the phone talking to someone he hoped was with the Asheville Police.

Charlie listened into the phone. "Haley?" He didn't hear a sound. "Haley?" He looked at the screen. They were still connected. "Haley?" he said, louder this time.

Frank turned when he heard him, then walked over to Charlie and Kim. "What the hell's going on?"

They each had a phone to their ear, Kim talking, explaining the situation, at least as much as she knew, to whoever was on the other end.

Frank listened, turning to Charlie. "Is that her? The girl?"

Charlie looked at Frank but didn't answer. He said into the phone one more time. "Haley? Can you hear me? If you're there..." He looked at his phone's screen one more time. The call had been disconnected. He said to Frank, "I gotta get up there." He glanced at his phone one more time. "Jesus Christ." He started toward the Suburban.

"Charlie," Frank said, loud enough for Charlie to hear him. "Will you tell me what the hell you're doing? What about Keegan?"

"I'm sorry, Frank," Charlie said, climbing up into the Suburban.

Kim yelled toward Charlie, "That was Billy. He's on his way over there," she said.

Charlie closed the door and started the engine, shifting into drive with one hand, dialing Haley's number with the hand he held the wheel with. He took off, heading north, and put the phone on speaker as he hit Route 26. He pushed the pedal to the floor and the engine roared, cutting into the oncoming traffic, yanking the wheel to the left lane.

The phone rang twice, a third ring, fourth… five times without an answer. Halfway into the sixth, it went to voicemail. The message came on and it wasn't Haley, just the automated voice reading off the number. The phone beeped and Charlie left a message.

"Haley, it's Charlie Harlow. Listen, if you hear this message, call me back. I'm on my way up there. Asheville Police'll be there any second, so just sit tight. But call me…" He hesitated, quiet, like he wasn't sure what to say. He knew she might not *hear* the message. "Or send me a text. Just let me know everything's all right." He hung up, his throat dryer than it had ever been, feeling his heart pound in his throat like it was going to bust open.

For someone who normally maintained better control, his nerves had gotten the best of him. Part of it was due to the fact he felt responsible, not doing enough to persuade Haley to find somewhere else to go. He thought about the Redhouse brothers while going ninety-seven miles per hour without even noticing the cars he passed, like they were practically standing still.

Charlie dialed the phone again, this time calling Lindsey at the Coyote Grille.

She answered on the third ring. "I was wondering when you were going to call me," she said with a somewhat jovial tone.

"Listen," Charlie said. "Have you seen or heard anything else from those two brothers?"

"Who?"

"Dillon and Jessie Redhouse. Have you seen them? Any chance they were in there again?"

She laughed. "Funny you should ask. They came in a few hours ago, both of 'em apologizing for the trouble they caused."

"No shit?"

"I know. It doesn't sound like something they'd do. But they did."

"Were they drinking?"

"Couple of beers." She went quiet for a moment. "Is everything all right, Charlie? You sound like—"

"They say anything else about that girl at the shopping center? The one they were talking about when I was in there?"

"Not to me. No. It was busy when they were here, so I didn't pay them much attention. Is everything all right?"

"The girl, her name's Haley. I actually spoke with her, gave her my cell phone number. She just called me, scared, hiding. She said the two brothers—Jessie and Dillon—were over there last night. At least she thinks they were." He had to cut the wheel into the right lane to move around a truck. A light rain had started to come down on the windshield. "You know what time they left?"

"Dustin and Jessie?" She paused. "I don't know. Maybe an hour ago?"

"An hour? Are you sure?" He looked at the clock on the radio.

"I told you, it was busy, Charlie. I don't know. I'd say, yes, probably left about an hour ago."

"They say where they were going? Anything about that girl? Or the Fillmore Shopping Center?"

"Jesus, Charlie. Are you all right? What—"

"She called me. Something's happened to her. It might be Dustin and Jessie, but I don't know. She didn't know."

"Oh my God," Lindsey said. "Is she all right?"

The noise in the background coming from the phone's speaker was loud, voices and music combined with clinking glasses almost covering over her voice.

"I don't know if she's all right," he said, shifting into the left lane again, then stuck behind a small car going too slow. He flashed his high beams and blasted the horn. The car moved out of his way, and he had the Suburban up to a hundred.

She said, "Where are you now?"

"On my way back from Hendersonville, letting another fugitive slip away."

Chapter 7

Charlie drove into the shopping center and stopped behind the three Asheville Police vehicles. Four officers stood in a circle between their vehicles, talking among each other—a couple drinking out of take-out cups—and didn't seem too concerned about doing much of anything else.

Charlie didn't like it when he saw one of the officers laughing, like he was having a good ol' time. He stepped down from his Suburban, kept it running, and walked toward them. "Don't strain yourselves looking for the missing girl."

A couple of the officers cleared their throats.

"Hey, Charlie," one of them said. It was Billy Leader, an officer with Asheville whom Charlie had known for at least ten years. "We haven't had much luck."

"No luck, huh? You gonna wait around in your little circle jerk, hoping a horseshoe's gonna hit you in the ass?"

"Come on, Charlie. We've been looking all over. Chief Brayden's on his way here now to make a plan as to how we're going to approach this."

Charlie took off his hat and pushed his hair back on his head, turning to look toward the fountain down the far end of the courtyard from where they stood. He looked at his phone, hoping any second he'd have a phone call from Haley. "In case you all don't have the complete story just yet, this young lady, Haley Moore, has been living out here in the shopping center, right down near the fountain. Sleeps here every night."

Billy nodded. "We know who she is. People call all the time, concerned, and tell us to help her out. But there's only so much we can do."

Charlie nodded, still looking toward the fountain. "Yeah, that's what I've been told."

One of the other officers spoke up. "Doesn't sound to me you did much about it, Charlie."

Charlie knew who the officer was but didn't even remember his name. He looked like a kid, young and skinny with a cocky look on his face. Charlie thought about popping him one, teach him a lesson, but quickly thought better of it. "You're right about that," he said, turning to Billy. "Did Kim tell you Dustin and Jessie Redhouse could've had something to do with it?"

"Chief Holden said Frank had called about her last night. But, like I said, most of us knew she'd been sleeping out here." He looked around the area. "Hopefully she's all right, Charlie."

"Hopefully." Charlie looked toward Cabo's Mexican Grille. "She was hiding behind a dumpster, back of the building over there behind the restaurant. I'm guessing you've already looked around back there?"

Billy Leader seemed to hesitate. "We've scoured the whole shopping center, Charlie. We're not done. We're just—"

"You telling me you already looked around that dumpster? In that wooded area over there?"

Billy looked at the others and nodded. "Yes. We're just hoping she's all right, maybe just took off, maybe dropped her phone, or—"

"Jesus, Billy. That's the second time you've used the word 'hope' while the four of you stand around with your dicks in your hands."

"Hey, Charlie, you don't need to be acting like that. You know we—"

"Enjoy those coffees," he said, stepping up into the Suburban he'd left running and slamming the door closed. He squealed the tires as he took off, if anything just to let the other law enforcement officials know he wasn't screwing around.

Charlie knocked on the door of a small one-story home with a dirt driveway and overgrown shrubs on either side of the front steps. It was past midnight, and over an hour had already passed since Haley had first called Charlie. Even an hour was too much time.

He knew two officers had already gone out to see Haley's dad, John Moore. The hope, of course, was she'd, by chance, gone home. But that didn't turn out to be the case. And Charlie hadn't gotten much out of the Asheville PD about what Mr. Moore had told them.

So he took it upon himself to find out, as he often did, and stepped up to the front door. He knocked, looking in through the panes of glass. The glow from a television filled a room down the hall and to the right.

The light on the exterior of the house, just up to the right of the door, came on. The front door opened, and a man older than Charlie, with gray, almost white, shoulder-length hair, stood in the doorway, staring out at him. He wore a robe with his skinny, bare legs coming out from under it.

"Yes?" the man said. "Who are *you*?"

Charlie got a whiff of marijuana coming from inside. "John Moore?"

The man seemed hesitant, looking past Charlie, then nodded. "Is there something I can—"

Charlie flashed his badge. "Deputy Charlie Harlow, with the U.S. Marshals Service."

"U.S. Marshals?"

Charlie nodded. "Yes, sir. I met Haley, yesterday. After overhearing someone mention she'd been sleeping down there at the Fillmore Shopping Center, I went over to talk to her. See if I could help."

The man's eyes had a red glow to them, his eyelids heavy. "I didn't know she'd been sleeping outside, you know. This is as much of a shock as..." He closed his eyes, rubbing his face with both hands. "I don't know what I'm supposed to do right now."

Smelling the weed smoke from the house, Charlie had a pretty good idea what Haley's dad had decided to do to deal with what had happened. Although he wasn't one for getting high, though he sure was when he was a kid, he understood everyone had different ways of dealing with shit that happened in life.

"So if Haley hasn't been here, where do you think she's been all this time?"

"With her boyfriend," John said. "She'd told me she was moving in with him."

"So you haven't seen her?"

John shook his head, again closing his eyes for a brief moment. "We haven't really spoken much at all in a few weeks."

"You have a fight or something?" Charlie said, suspicious now.

"I didn't want her moving in with that kid. Two young kids... no idea what life is all about."

"You didn't want her moving in with the boyfriend?"

"I told her she couldn't. But she did it anyway. At least last I knew she had. She took off, moved out while I was at work, and hasn't called me since."

"Have you called her?"

"Yes, but she never answered my calls or called me back."

Charlie gave him a curious look. "You didn't do anything else to talk to her? Go looking for her?"

John Moore didn't appear to like Charlie's question. "I don't need to be judged for my parenting skills right now," he said.

Charlie knew he was wrong for saying it. "I'm sorry. I'm just—"

"And you don't know Haley," he said. "You can't tell her anything. She's stubborn, like her mother."

"Is she here?" Charlie said. "Her mother?"

John paused, then said, "She died five years ago."

"I'm sorry," Charlie said.

Haley's dad appeared calm, but this time had a tear come down his face. "I feel helpless. The police that were here told me not to leave the house, in case she shows up. But I can't just sit here." He turned, looked back over his shoulder toward the hall behind him. "So the U.S. Marshals Service, huh? Are you helping the police?"

Charlie was hesitant to answer. It was still at a point where Charlie was on his own. He wasn't there representing the Marshals Service and wasn't in a position to tell the man he was. "There are a couple of young men, might've had something to do with her disappearance, and I might—"

"You mean you think she was kidnapped?" The man had a surprised look on his face Charlie wasn't expecting.

"What exactly did the officers tell you?" he said, realizing he'd let the cat out of the bag and maybe he wasn't supposed to. But he wasn't sure why.

"They just said they're looking for her. Didn't really give me a lot of details. Like I said, they told me to stay here and wait, in case she came home."

Charlie swallowed, not sure how to clearly explain the situation and why he'd gotten himself involved. It was like he couldn't help himself. "Well, the truth is we don't know exactly what happened. So I don't mean to jump to any conclusions, but I'd checked up on your daughter a couple of times, gave her the number to a woman's homeless shelter, and—"

"A homeless shelter?" John Moore ran his hand over his white head of hair and left it there, on top. "Why didn't someone come tell me she was in trouble? Why wouldn't you show up at my door before something happened?"

Charlie nodded, knowing the man wasn't wrong for thinking the way he was. "Well, sir, it all happened fast. Haley didn't seem to want anyone's help. I just... I wanted to help. I also gave her my card, told her to call me if she ever runs into trouble."

"So she called you?"

Charlie nodded.

"And she was in trouble?"

After a pause, Charlie nodded again, hesitant to admit what he believed to be true. "But the two young men I mentioned... I'm almost certain they know something about it."

"But, if she called you and said she was in trouble, why didn't you help her?"

Charlie shifted his stance, his hand on the back of his neck, looking down toward the concrete step. "Well, sir, I happened to be down on a case in Hendersonville when she called me. If I was closer... I would've been there right away. I drove up as fast as I could, let a fugitive slip away, so I could get back to Asheville to help her. I realize I was too late, but we're doing all we can. Asheville Police, as you know, have officers out there looking for her right now."

Haley's dad wiped the tears from his eyes. "So, what am I supposed to do?"

Exactly what the officers told you to do, just wait right here."

"I should call Jaylen," John said.

"Jaylen?" Charlie said.

"Her boyfriend. Or, he *was*, last I knew. I don't know what happened. As much as I hated she was moving in with him, she's not a kid anymore. She's old enough to make her own decisions."

"You really believe that?" Charlie said.

Mr. Moore shrugged.

Charlie said. "What's this kid's last name?"

"Beard. Jaylen Beard."

"Does he live around here?"

"He's from Weaverville."

Chapter 8

CHARLIE DIALED HIS PHONE from the Fillmore Shopping Center parking lot, and Frank answered on the first ring.

"I thought maybe you'd be asleep," Charlie said.

"I was, but I just got off the phone with Chief Brayden. And he wasn't happy, Charlie. What the hell were you thinking? Going over to this young lady's father's house before anybody had even told him what had happened? Do you have any idea what it's like being woken up by Brayden screaming in your ear at this time in the morning?"

"How was I supposed to know they didn't tell him the whole story? The man's daughter was likely abducted, Frank. You don't think he has a right to know?"

"You don't have a right to get involved in local police business, Charlie. How many times do I have to tell you, you can't just go off on your own, like you're some kind of—"

"I'm sorry, Frank. But, I mean, I came here earlier, and there's Billy, out here with three other officers standing around with their thumbs up their asses. I just thought maybe I could get some answers from the father."

"I told you when you first wanted to get involved, going to see this girl, you weren't on official duty of the U.S. Marshals Service. You still aren't. We have to let Asheville PD do their thing, Charlie. You understand?"

"Come on, Frank. You know how fast we gotta act when—"

"You can't help yourself; I realize that. But you gotta back off, Charlie. Asheville PD wants us involved, then that's a different story. They've got their men and women out there looking for her right now as we speak. But the problem we have right now—and all we have—is a call she made to you that got disconnected."

"Don't give me that, Frank. She's in trouble. She was scared, and told me the night before that the Redhouse brothers were over there."

Frank sighed into the phone. "But you don't know for sure it was them, Charlie. We have very little information. Certainly not enough for you to start ruffling Chief Brayden's feathers."

"Well, like I said. They didn't seem to be doing much when I came by here earlier."

"Where's 'here'?" he said. "Where are you now?"

"At the shopping center. I just took a drive through. There's nobody here. Wouldn't you think there'd be at least one officer out here, combing over the place?"

Frank paused, quiet on the other end. "They're looking for her, Charlie. I promise you. The way you're talking, it's like you don't think they give a shit."

"That's not what I'm saying," he said, stepping out from the Suburban.

"I assure you they're not all cuddled up at home in their beds like nothing happened. And speaking of, I need to get at least a couple hours sleep. You know how much I love sleeping in hotels."

"Where are you?"

"I'm still in Hendersonville, trying to clean up your other mess."

"Oh," Charlie said, walking over the footbridge toward the fountain. "I'd be surprised they're still in Hendersonville," he said. "Sorry about that."

The line was quiet, and Charlie could hear nothing else but the sounds coming from the fountain.

"You don't have to be sorry. But I do need you to remember you're a U.S. Marshal. You want to be a cop, maybe you should've thought of that long before."

"What's that supposed to mean?" Charlie said.

"I don't even know. But I'm tired. I'm an old man, so if you'd please let me get some sleep so I can think straight in the morning. "Is that too much to ask?"

Frank hung up, and Charlie tucked his phone in his pocket, continued toward the fountain and walked around to the other side, where the bench was where Haley had been sleeping when he first met her. He continued around the fountain and over toward Cabo's, walked past the entrance and around to the backside of the building. It was dark back there, with a strong garbage-like odor floating in the air. He spotted the dumpster with a spotlight shining down from the building's brick exterior above.

Billy Leader had told Charlie they'd looked around the dumpster, but he got the feeling by the way everyone was acting, they might've thought Haley wasn't in trouble as Charlie had said. Maybe they thought she was just another junkie, hiding out, doing drugs back there. Maybe that's why nobody seemed to be taking her disappearance as seriously as Charlie felt they should.

On the other hand, Charlie had no idea what Haley was up to. He didn't know much about her at all. Her father looked the part himself, at home smoking pot, hanging around in nothing but a robe, like the junkies Charlie'd come across dozens of times before.

He removed his flashlight from his belt and looked down around the dumpster. Even if the area had been covered by Asheville PD, as Billy had claimed, it never hurt to look twice.

A thought came to him as he took out his phone and tapped the number Haley had called him from. He'd already tried calling her a dozen times and all it ever did was ring five or six times before going to voicemail.

With phone to ear, he listened as the call connected. It started to ring, but the ringing he heard wasn't coming through the phone. The sound came from somewhere nearby where he stood.

He held the phone away from his ear to listen, but the faint ringing he heard had stopped. He looked around, dialed her number again, and crouched down, getting lower to the ground. As soon as he realized it wasn't coming from the immediate area around the dump-ster, where he stood, the ringing once again stopped. He walked toward the wooded area, dialing her num-ber. The ringing was louder now as he stepped into the woods. He turned off his flashlight and spotted a glow coming up from under the leaves, ten feet away from him. He hurried over to it and reached down, picking up the ringing phone. He looked through the trees and out toward another parking lot beyond the wooded area.

Charlie looked at the screen on her phone but it was locked with a passcode. He saw there were missed texts and twenty-three missed calls, at least a dozen from Charlie himself. He slipped the phone in his pocket and turned his flashlight on again, shining the light along the ground. He continued through the woods toward the parking lot on the other side. He hated to think the officers who were on the scene hadn't even searched the wooded area. It made no sense.

He moved the flashlight slowly, from left to right, covering as much ground as possible, wondering what else the officers may have overlooked. Stepping out from the wooded area and into the empty parking lot, he looked out toward a car parked far away at the other end. His phone rang as he started to turn back toward the woods.

He looked at the screen and saw it was Kim.

"Hey," he said, walking through the woods with the phone up to his ear, the flashlight aimed toward the ground.

"Where are you?" she said.

"The shopping center. I just found Haley Moore's phone."

"You found it? How?"

"In the woods, right nearby where she told me she was, buried under some leaves. And here I am, getting shit for saying the cops hadn't done a thing yet."

"I'm not sure that's true," she said. "I know for a fact they're out there looking for her."

"Well, they missed a pretty big clue," he said, using his hand with the flashlight to push twigs out of his way.

"If you promise not to tell Frank, I have an address for you, up in Weaverville. The Redhouse brothers have an aunt, used to live up there in a mobile home community, but she's been in a nursing facility for the past two months after suffering a stroke. She owns the property, and I'd say it's a good guess they could be living out there."

"What do you know about her? Why would they be living in her house?"

"Her name's on their court records, from when they were minors."

Charlie looked toward the dumpster, nodding. "Worth a shot."

Charlie turned right off Jupiter Hill Road after passing the brown wooden sign for Pleasant View Mobile Home Community, drove a quarter of a mile and went left, onto Clover Brook Drive. It was dark with plenty of trees on either side of the road, no streetlights. He drove past a dozen homes, most with lights on inside, and stopped when he saw the number twenty-two on the mailbox.

He turned down the dirt driveway, had his window cracked and could smell burning wood from somewhere outside. Parked in front of him was a rusty Ford Bronco II with faded black paint. He looked at the registration number he'd written down and confirmed right then it belonged to Jessie Redhouse.

He stepped out, gently closed the driver's-side door without letting it make a sound, and walked down the sloped driveway, his feet crunching on the dirt and stone.

The smell of smoke was stronger, and he saw the glow coming from what looked like a firepit someone had built just outside the door. He walked over and looked down at the orange embers. There were four folding lawn chairs placed around the firepit, although the webbing on one of the chairs was torn at the seat. At least a dozen beer cans littered the dirt ground.

Charlie looked in through the windows on the home, didn't see a single light on inside. The bulb on the vinyl exterior, to the right of the door, was out.

Charlie was surrounded by quiet and darkness. "Jessie? Dustin? You out here?" He had a pretty good feeling they were hiding, and wondered what they might do. He walked back toward the Bronco II and placed his hand on the cold hood. But maybe the Bronco didn't run.

He went back to the Suburban and grabbed his flashlight from under the front seat, shining it into the woods and toward either side of the home as he walked back down the driveway to the front door.

He waited a moment, trying to listen for a sound before he knocked on the frame of the aluminum screen door. He yelled through the door, "Jessie! Dustin! You in there? It's Deputy Harlow, from Coyote Grille. If you're in there, I'd like to talk to you. You're not in any kind of trouble."

Not yet, at least.

He waited, listening.

Something snapped in the woods, and Charlie put his hand on his Glock, still holstered, and turned the flashlight toward the right, moving it back and forth along the trees. "Jessie? Dustin? You boys come out here. I just want to talk." He didn't move a muscle, his eyes following the flashlight's beam.

Everything was quiet.

He thought he heard something inside the house and quickly turned the flashlight toward the window to his left, shining it through the glass. He saw nothing.

He walked around to the back of the home and came around to the front again, reaching for his phone. He turned off the flashlight and stood over the firepit, look-ing at what was left of the fire.

He tapped the screen and placed the phone up to his ear.

The phone rang twice and Billy Leader answered.

"Charlie?"

"Hey, Billy. Sorry to call you so late. I just wanted to check, make sure you didn't by chance come across either of the Redhouse brothers yet, have you?"

Billy was quiet for a moment on the other end. "Sorry, Charlie. I would've let you know if we had. We've looked everywhere for them so far. Police up in Weaverville have done the same."

"I'm actually up in Weaverville right now. At the aunt's house."

"The aunt's house?" he said. "I didn't know they had an aunt up there."

Charlie didn't want to give Billy a harder time than he already had. He knew he meant well, and was a decent cop, for the most part. "Well, I got a lead and thought I'd come check it out. I guess the aunt had to be put in some kind of nursing home, or something like it. The boys must be staying here, but there's no sign of 'em anywhere."

Charlie thought he saw something in the window and put his face up against it, trying to see inside. Billy said something he hadn't quite heard.

What he did hear, and sure as hell felt, was the crack of something hard against the back of his head. He stumbled forward and turned just as a two-by-four piece of wood was coming down at him again.

But he lifted both hands and caught it two inches from cracking him on the side of his head.

His phone dropped into the firepit.

He recognized the young man holding the other end of the wood as Jessie, yanking it from his grasp. He swung it and hit Jessie in the side of the head, knocking him out cold.

The Bronco's engine started up, and the headlights shot right toward Charlie standing over Jessie down in the dirt, holding his head.

Charlie reached down into the firepit for his phone, burning his hand in the process, and ran toward the Bronco. He couldn't see who was behind the wheel but had no doubt it was Jessie's brother, Dustin.

Charlie had his Glock out and raised it toward the windshield but decided to go for the front tire. He squeezed the trigger and fired a shot that hit the wheel on the driver's side. He took aim again and hit the back rear tire on the same side.

The Bronco's wheels turned, kicking up sand and stones as it spun around and headed for the road.

Charlie looked back at Jessie whimpering on the ground and took off, running after the Bronco.

But the driver didn't get far.

The Bronco crashed head-on into a tree no more than thirty yards away.

Charlie kept running, heading across the street toward it. But by the time he got there, the driver—assuming it was Dustin— had already jumped out and disappeared into the woods.

Steam blew out from under the Bronco II's hood.

Charlie rushed back over to Jessie, rolled him over onto his stomach and slapped the handcuffs on his wrists. He read him his rights and lifted him by one arm to his feet.

Jessie was half out of it, his head rolling on his shoulders, but he was good enough to walk, with Charlie's help, back to the Suburban.

Charlie tossed him into the back passenger seat and slammed the door but then had to grab on to the side of the Suburban to hold himself up. A woozy feeling came over him as he made it to the driver's-side door and slipped in behind the wheel. He reached for the back of his head and felt the sticky warmth of his own blood.

He flipped on the interior light and looked at his hand, covered in blood.

He turned the key in the ignition and slapped it into reverse but kept his foot on the brake for a moment, squeezing his eyes tight to get some focus. He felt the back of his head again, his hair coming out from under his cap, wet with blood. Taking his foot off the brake, he backed up onto the road. The Suburban's headlights shined on the Bronco as he shifted into drive and turned the wheel. But he stopped and slammed the shifter into park. His vision was blurred.

He felt his damp, clammy forehead and closed his eyes as his head fell forward, resting against the top of the steering wheel. Within seconds, Charlie had lost consciousness.

Chapter 9

BILLY LEADER STOOD OUTSIDE the Suburban talking, Charlie hearing his voice but having a hard time getting his eyes to open. He jumped, startled, like someone waking from a bad dream. "What the hell's going on?" he said.

The area in front of the Redhouse brothers' aunt's house was well lit with the searchlight from Billy's police vehicle shining toward the Suburban, parked crooked and half in the road where Charlie had left it.

Charlie squinted, holding up his hand to block the light. He looked into the empty back seat. "Where the hell's Jessie?" He felt the back of his head. "Son of a bitch got away."

Sirens could be heard in the distance, growing louder.

Billy eased him against the backrest. "Rescue's on its way," he said. "You'll be all right, Charlie."

Charlie pushed his way past Billy as he stepped out from the car. "When did you get here?"

"Fifteen minutes after I lost you on the phone. I had a feeling something was wrong. I called Deputy Marshal Riggins to get the exact address. I knew something was up." Billy went to his car and grabbed a towel from the front seat. "You're going to need to get that sewn up," he said, nodding toward Charlie's head and handing him the towel.

"It's fine," he said, looking around toward the woods. "Jessie Redhouse came up behind me with a two-by-four, caught me just right. He pressed the towel against the back of his head. "I didn't even know I was bleeding. At least at first."

A Chevy Tahoe parked behind the Suburban, blocking half the road. It was Kim Riggins. "Are you okay?" she said, pulling her blue U.S. Marshal jacket over her T-shirt.

It had gotten colder since Charlie first showed up at the aunt's house.

He nodded. "I'm all right."

"I'm going to have to disagree," Billy said. "He was passed out when I got here, his face against the steering wheel."

"I was resting," Charlie said, still looking out toward the woods. "I don't know how far they could've gotten, but they're out there."

Kim came up behind him, pulling his hand holding the towel on the back of his head, away. She studied his wound. "That's a pretty good one."

The sirens grew louder, red lights coming through the trees now.

Charlie looked at Billy. "What'd you call them for?"

The rescue vehicle stopped in the road behind Kim's Tahoe, floodlights shining toward the top of the driveway, where Kim and Billy stood with Charlie.

A man and a woman jumped down from the truck and hurried over. "You the one who's hurt?" the man said, looking Charlie over.

Charlie held out the bloody towel. "I was, but I'm all right now. Sorry for wasting your time."

The woman grabbed him by the arm and took his hat off his head. She shined a flashlight on him from behind. "Oh, yeah. That's a good one. Any other injuries?"

Charlie shook his head but winced when he did. His head had started to pound. He didn't feel quite as dizzy as he had but wasn't feeling quite himself, either. "It's not that bad, is it?"

The female paramedic nodded, looking at the other like she wanted his opinion. She kept the light shined on the back of Charlie's head as the male with her studied it from behind.

The man said, "Why don't you come with us; we'll drive you over to Mission Emergency, get you all cleaned up."

Charlie took his hat back from the woman's hand, placed it gently on his head. "You really think it's that bad?"

All four nodded, standing around Charlie.

Kim said, "We all know you're a tough guy, Charlie. But maybe knock it off for the time being, take a ride, and get yourself taken care of." She walked over to his Suburban and looked at his seat. The light from the vehicles shined inside. "That's a lot of blood in there."

Charlie said, "How about I drive myself over?" He nodded toward the Suburban. "I can't leave that here."

Kim put out her hand. "Give me your keys. I'll move it for you." She nodded toward the two paramedics. "You all right, if I drive him there?"

They both exchanged a glance and nodded. "Just make sure you take him right there," the woman said.

———

Charlie walked through the automatic double doors from the trauma center at Mission Hospital's ER. He had a bandage on the back of his head, the area around it shaved down to the skin.

Kim got up from the chair looking like she'd fallen asleep. "You all right?" she said, checking her watch as she yawned.

"You didn't have to hang around," he said.

She nodded, giving him a grin. "I know." She put her hand on his back as the two walked through the sliding glass doors.

"Twenty-one stitches," he said, turning to her. "And a slight concussion."

"Oh," she said. "And you were going to do, what, just go home and sleep it off?" She let out a slight laugh, shaking her head.

"You talk to Frank?" he said.

"Of course. He's not happy."

"You told him what I was doing up there?"

Kim pointed her key fob at her maroon Tahoe, parked near the entrance under a streetlight. "Should I have lied to him?"

"Well," Charlie said, leaving it at that as he stepped around to the passenger side. "You mind taking me back up to get the Suburban?"

They both got in the Tahoe. "The doctor said you shouldn't drive."

Charlie put on his seat belt, staring at Kim. "I leave it up there overnight, those Redhouse brothers are going to strip it down to pieces, if they haven't already. Or burn it."

Kim started the engine and backed out of the space. "Weaverville PD's looking for them both right now. Billy's still up there, as are a couple deputies from the sheriff's office."

"No sign yet?"

"Of the brothers?"

Charlie nodded. "Or Haley?"

Kim shook her head, turning from the hospital parking lot onto Biltmore Ave. "I do believe it's being taken a little more seriously at this point," she said. "At least it looks that way."

"Oh, so you agree with me now?" he said.

"About *what*? That it wasn't being taken seriously?"

He reached into his pocket and pulled out two phones. One was Haley's. "I didn't know if I should've given this to Billy."

Kim gave him a quick glance. "Her phone?"

"I'm not sure we can even get into it, or if there's anything on here anyway."

Kim turned onto Lexington and headed for Interstate 26.

"Has anybody collected footage from the shopping center? The night she was abducted?"

Kim didn't answer right away. "I think you need to talk to Frank, Charlie. I know you want to be involved, but—"

"But what? He doesn't want me to help find a young woman? These two clowns. All we have to do is find these two clowns, the brothers, and let's just pray they didn't harm her in any way. If you know what I'm saying."

"The police are handling it, Charlie. And now the sheriff's office is involved."

"Is this you talking? Or Frank?"

"He's still pissed James Keegan got away."

"More important than a girl who's missing?"

Kim said, "You'll have to talk to Frank. I'm not the one making the calls here."

Charlie was quiet, watching out the window as they passed the Fairfield Inn and Suites near downtown. He thought about stopping to see Lyndsey after he got the Suburban, instead of driving out to Swannanoa and sleeping alone.

Kim took the exit for NC-197 toward Jupiter. "How bad was Jessie Redhouse hurt?" she said, turning left onto Flat Creek School Road.

Charlie turned from the window. "I thought worse than me, at least at first. He was barely conscious when I put the cuffs on him, threw him in back. I can't imagine

Dustin showing up. Last I saw him, he was running full speed, deep into the woods."

"After he drove the Bronco into the tree?"

Charlie sighed, shaking his head. "It wasn't long ago, kid like Dustin wouldn't have a chance of getting away."

"You mean because in the past you would have shot him?"

"Nah. I'm just slowing down. Getting old."

Kim laughed. "What are you, thirty-seven? I'd hardly call that old."

"Well, old enough I can't catch a twenty-one-year-old kid who just drove into a tree."

They turned into Jessie and Dustin's aunt's home, Charlie's Suburban still in the driveway where Kim had moved it before they left for the hospital.

"I thought you said the cops were out here looking for them?" He looked through the beams from the headlights.

"We don't know where they are right now," she said. "But they're out there. They went through the aunt's house, but didn't find anything." She gave Charlie a look, like she had something she wanted to say but wasn't sure how to say it.

"What?" he said. "Go ahead, you can say it."

"You have to have a little more faith," she said. "In our law enforcement partners."

"Who said I didn't have faith? It's just that—"

"Charlie," she said. "I'm serious. It's not going to fly this time. Frank won't let it."

"So I'm just supposed to walk away?" He turned, looking out the window into the woods along the aunt's property. "It might be different if I didn't feel somewhat responsible for what's happened." He turned to her. "You know what I'm saying?"

She nodded, her lips tight together. She put out her hand. "You want me to see what I can do with her phone?"

Charlie handed it to her and grinned. "I won't say a word."

———

Charlie rolled over in Lindsey's bed, reaching for his phone on the side table next to him. It was six in the morning, three hours after he showed up at her apartment looking for a little sympathy.

He'd slept for two and a half hours.

As soon as he sat up on the edge of the bed, looking at his phone, Lindsey rested her hand on his naked back. "Why are you up so early?"

He turned to look at her, feeling the bandage on the back of his head. "I think I might head into the office."

She yawned, turned, and looked at the clock behind her. "Don't you think you should rest today? After what you've been through?"

He shook his head. "Why?"

"You told me yourself, the doctor said you had a mild concussion. On top of all those stitches."

He stood from the bed and grabbed his pants from the floor, pulling them up to his waist. It was too dark in the room to see his shirt. "You mind I turn the lamp on?"

She said, "Don't you think you should rest."

"I gotta get in before Frank. He's not too happy about what happened." He turned on the lamp.

Lindsey shielded her eyes, squinting. "Because you got hurt?"

"I don't think he cares about that. He doesn't want me involved in something the Marshals Service isn't technically supposed to be involved with right now."

Lindsey sat up, her legs folded in front of her with her arms hugging her knees.

"I thought you said the U.S. Marshals have a whole division that has to do with kids being abducted."

"We do," he said. "But Haley Moore's not a kid. Not technically anyway. She's what you'd call a young woman who could slip through the cracks."

"But aren't the police out there looking for her?"

Charlie saw his shirt sticking out from under the bed. It was covered in dried blood, but he slipped it on anyway, being careful not to rip the bandage from the back of his head.

"You have a shirt in the closet," Lindsey said, stepping down from the bed. She had on a T-shirt, a long one that came down just above her knees. Charlie knew she had nothing else underneath.

She opened the closet door and reached in, pulled out a button-down shirt on a hanger. "This is yours, right?"

Charlie stared at it. He wasn't sure it was, and for a moment it felt a little weird to him. He stepped over, took it from her, and looked it over, checking the size on the tag. "It'll do," he said, removing his bloodstained shirt. He slipped the new one on.

Lindsey walked over and rubbed his chest, felt his muscular abs, then helped him button it, leaning in to give him a kiss. "I wish you'd be more careful out there," she said.

For a second, Charlie thought about Jennie, his ex. She said it to him all the time after he'd come home banged up until she couldn't take it anymore and asked for a divorce.

Lindsey gave him a kiss, then Charlie turned away, went in the bathroom to clean up, and headed for the door a few minutes later.

"So you really think Jessie and Dustin are the ones who took her?" She shook her head. "I know they've got their troubles, but I just don't picture either one of 'em for kidnappers."

Charlie fixed his cap on his head but didn't like the way it rubbed against his covered wound. He took it off again and felt the area where they shaved his head. "We gotta find them, first," he said.

"But, I'm just saying," Lindsey said. "What if you find them and they know nothing about it? Shouldn't you be looking in another direction? Just in case?"

Charlie liked Lindsey. She was smart. Maybe not book-smart like Jennie, but street smart. She had a good head on her shoulders, full of common sense. But he didn't love it when she offered up her unsolicited advice.

"Well, like I said, I have a feeling Frank's going to put the clamps on me, maybe even send me out of town after the fugitive I let slip away." He gave her a quick kiss. "Thanks."

"For what?" she said, watching Charlie as he turned and walked out the door.

Chapter 10

CHARLIE SAT AT HIS desk at the office, on the third floor of the courthouse in Asheville. He had the overhead fluorescents turned off, his laptop's screen glowing on his face the only other light coming from the small, dim glass lamp he got from his grandmother's house after she died.

He looked up from his laptop when he heard the door to the office open, just a few feet away from his cubicle. He squinted when whoever it was turned on the bright overhead lights.

"Charlie? Is that you over there?" It was Frank, and he poked his head over the gray divider. "You doing all right?"

Charlie swiveled in the chair, turning from his desk to face him. "I think so."

Frank tried to look at the back of Charlie's head. "Kim said he got you pretty good."

Charlie touched the bandage, although he wondered if he could just pull it off. "I've had worse."

Frank stepped to the opening of Charlie's cubicle and leaned against the edge of it, one hand in his pocket, the other holding a tall cup of coffee. He took a sip and said, "Sheriff Cobb's coming over this morning, wants to meet with us." He looked at his watch. "About nine."

"Sheriff Cobb, huh? You know what about?"

Frank glanced at the floor. "Well, until I heard from him this morning, I was ready to come in here and tear you a new one. But, it turns out the sheriff's office may be taking over the missing persons case."

"You mean, Haley Moore?"

Frank nodded. "I don't know for sure how it all materialized the way it did. May be just political, or administrative, considering the search is countywide."

"What search?" Charlie said. "I haven't gotten much of an indication anyone at all's been looking for her."

"I know they didn't seem to be moving as fast as you would've liked, but I promise you, Chief Brayden wasn't just sitting on his hands."

Charlie and Chief Brayden didn't always see eye to eye, and having him hand off the investigation was good news to him, as long as the sheriff was willing to have Charlie involved.

It sounds to me Brayden was the one who first initiated it, after the way things went down last night."

"With me?" Charlie said.

"Well, you and the Redhouse brothers. With the two of them out on the loose, and—did you see the news last night?"

Charlie shook his head. He couldn't remember the last time he watched TV, unless he was at the bar. "Did I miss something?"

"John Moore, Haley's father, was making threats against Asheville PD, talking about getting a lawyer, how he didn't think anyone was taking it seriously."

"I guess I'm not the only one," Charlie said.

"He mentioned you," Frank said. "Not personally. Just that a U.S. Marshal who stopped by his house seemed to be the only one who gave a damn." He gave Charlie a quick nod. "Sheriff asked me if it was you."

Charlie rubbed the stubble on his face. "Is that why he's coming here?"

Frank said, "Our resources are as thin as they've ever been, but he asked me to include you in the meeting. If he wants our help, I told him he'll get it." He looked at his watch and sipped his coffee. "So don't be late." Frank turned and walked away without another word.

Charlie heard the main door open again at the front of the office, poked his head up over the cubicle wall and saw Kim walking toward him.

She had a phone in her hand, and Charlie thought maybe it was Haley's. With a quick glance toward Frank's office, she kept her voice low, like she didn't want Frank to hear. She handed Charlie the phone. "You see your email?"

"No, why? You send me something?"

"I got someone to crack the phone. You can open it now, but we downloaded whatever photos she had on there."

"Who's 'we'?" Charlie said.

"I have my sources," she said. "Just check your email. I uploaded the photos; wait'll you see what's on there. You should have the link." She glanced over her shoulder toward Frank's office. "Take a look. Did you even tell Frank you found her phone?"

"Not yet," Charlie said.

"Well, once you see those photos, you have to tell him what's up. I'm sure he'll ask you... tell you to take that phone over to Asheville PD. He's not going to allow you to—"

"I don't think we have to worry about that," Charlie said, typing in his password to open his email. He rarely checked it and wasn't sure the last time he'd even opened it up. He leaned closer to the screen, squinting, as he looked for the email Kim had sent, then clicked on the link. Right away he saw at least forty or fifty photos open up on the screen. The ones in the top row were somewhat blurry and dark, but you could just about make out a man's face, almost like it was up close. The angle was odd, as if the photos were shot from the ground, facing toward the sky. It looked to Charlie like there were branches in front of the man's face, but it was hard to make out exactly what it was.

Kim waited just outside Charlie's cubicle, watching him stare at his screen. She said, "If you look at it close enough, doesn't it look like she might've gotten off a couple of pictures... almost as if it's of someone walking after her? The angle... even the branches in the photos... looks like she's in a wooded area. And there's a building in the background, but it's too blurry to see what it is."

Charlie looked closer, studying the photos in front of him without saying much at first. He pointed at the building. "I'd say *this* right here is that Mexican place, Cabo's." He turned and looked at Kim over his shoulder. "That's right by where I found her phone, maybe twenty feet away."

Kim nodded. "You think there's a chance she left that phone behind, Charlie? Maybe hoping you or someone else would find it?"

Charlie had printed out the photos Kayla had gotten from Haley's phone, slipped them into a manila folder and carried them over to Frank's office.

Sheriff Cobb was due there any moment.

Charlie knocked on Frank's open door. "Chief?" he said as Frank looked up.

Nobody around the office called Frank "Chief" unless they were either being reprimanded by him or they were in the presence of other law enforcement officials, especially the higher-ups like Sheriff Cobb.

Charlie held the closed folder down by his side. "I've got something to show you. Something we'll want to share with Sheriff Cobb, whenever he shows up. I'm assuming he's going to be bringing us on board."

"Even if he's not," Frank said "I hope you're not trying to suggest you'd withhold any kind of information."

"That's not exactly what I said." Charlie dropped the folder in front of Frank, on his desk. "Take a look," he said. "These came off Haley Moore's phone."

Frank removed his reading glasses, looking up at Charlie in the doorway. "Haley Moore's phone? Where'd you get—"

"Just look at the photos, Frank. We can get into the details of it all later."

"Please don't tell me you went and got somebody to crack open another phone without going through the proper channels, Charlie."

Kim passed by the office, and Frank gave her a look, like he knew she likely had helped Charlie, as she always did.

"Deputy Riggins," Frank said, holding up the first photo in the folder before he even looked at it. "Did you have anything to do with this?"

Kim just kept walking, like she was in a hurry and didn't hear him.

Frank shook his head as he slipped his glasses back on and studied the first photo he saw. "Who is this?"

"We don't know," Charlie said. "Hard to make out the face, but there's a good chance whoever it is had something to do with what happened to Haley."

Frank said, "This doesn't look like either of the Redhouse brothers, does it?" He placed the photos down on his desk and spread them out, one next to the other, looking over each in turn.

"That's the thing," Charlie said. "It's not. Neither one of them. I'd say whoever it is *may* be around the same age, but that's about it."

"Didn't she tell you it was them when she called you?"

"She didn't know who it was. Honestly, Frank, I—"

"Jesus, Charlie. You go off on your own little man-hunt after these two, and you weren't even sure it was them?"

"If you want to consider me going to their aunt's house, going on a 'manhunt,' so be it."

"You know what I'm saying."

Charlie looked down at the floor. "Nobody else was doing anything about looking for these two. Or looking for Haley Moore, for that matter. So…"

Frank nodded. "You seem to forget, as a deputy U.S. Marshal, your job is to—"

"I know what my job entails, Frank." He threw up his hands and started to walk from the office.

"Charlie, get your ass back in here," he said. "Don't be getting all sensitive on me, all right? I'm just saying, every time you decide to go rogue, it's my ass that ends up in the sling. One of these days I'll stop trying to cover up for you. I won't give a damn *what* you do."

Charlie leaned against the frame of the door, his arms crossed. "It doesn't mean the Redhouse brothers had nothing to do with it," he said.

Frank nodded. "I guess I'd agree with that."

Charlie said, "Can't we send the digital files out to intelligence, see if they can come up with a match?"

"We're not doing anything further until we've met with Sheriff Cobb." He looked at Charlie over the rim of his glasses. "Am I clear?"

"Crystal."

Frank gathered up the photos and slid them back into the folder.

Charlie said, "We were thinking there's a good chance Haley took these photos, knowing someone was after her."

"Who's 'we'?" Frank said.

Charlie didn't have to answer.

"Do you have to drag Deputy Riggins in with you every time you get involved in something you're not supposed to?" Frank said. He handed Charlie the folder. "You really think she would've taken photos like this, knowing she was about to be abducted?"

"It's also possible she might've dropped her phone on purpose, hoping someone like me would pick it up."

Frank leaned with his arms folded in front of him. "Smart kid?"

Charlie nodded, turned from the door, and went back to his desk.

Sheriff Ross Cobb of the Buncombe County Sheriff's Office sat with Deputy Carl Ryan to his left. Frank, Kim, and Charlie sat on the opposite side of the table.

"Chief Brayden isn't turning his back on the case," the sheriff said, "but he believes my office is in a better position to take over, while the search and investigation is just getting started."

"Just getting started?" Charlie said. "No disrespect to him, but we lost at least twenty-four hours waiting for Chief Brayden's men to 'get started.'" He held up the phone. "What kind of search overlooks a cell phone, sitting right there in the woods, twenty feet from where I told them Haley had called me from."

Frank was giving Charlie a look like he'd crossed the line, but for whatever reason chose to bite his tongue. "What Charlie's trying to say," Frank said, turning to Sheriff Cobb, "is you're already starting behind the eight ball. I'm not going to disagree with him about that."

"Well," the sheriff said, "that's why we're hoping you have the capacity to assist us, not only in finding this young woman, but bringing whoever is responsible to justice."

Frank nodded, looking at Charlie. "I don't think you'll have to ask him twice." He leaned on the table toward Kim. "I can give you Deputy Riggins, and anyone else I can free up."

Charlie pointed toward the folder with the photos from Haley's phone. "You want us to run the original files through intelligence on our end? We can see what we can come up with, see if we can get some kind of ID."

The sheriff opened the folder and looked over the photos a second time. "And you're sure this isn't one of the two brothers?"

"Just because they're not in either of those photos doesn't mean they had nothing to do with her abduction. But, no, the man in that photo is neither Jessie nor Dustin Redhouse."

The sheriff picked up the ziplock bag with Haley's phone inside it. "I'm sorry for asking, Charlie, but I'm not exactly clear on why you didn't give this to Asheville PD?"

"I thought you just said the sheriff's office was taking over?" Charlie said.

"But you didn't know that last night, when you found it," the sheriff said.

Frank said, "Charlie was incapacitated, Sheriff." He pointed at the back of Charlie's head. "He would have, if he hadn't taken a two-by-four off the skull that knocked him out cold." As much as Frank liked to give Charlie shit, he stood up for Charlie, and any other deputy under his command, whenever he felt it was necessary. He cleared his throat. "If it's all right with you, I'd say let's just move past what's happened up till this point. The U.S. Marshals Service is here to help you any way we can. Just give us the word."

Charlie's phone rang, and he reached into his pocket to pull it out. He took a quick glance at the screen. He had a feeling he knew whose number it was and answered, "This is Deputy Harlow." Charlie put the call on speaker and placed it down on the table so everyone else could hear.

"This is Jaylen Beard. I had a couple of messages from you last night?"

"Thanks for returning my call, Jaylen. I'm sure you know why I'm calling?"

"Yeah, of course. Is Haley all right?"

Charlie glanced at the others, watching him. "We hope so," he said. "But we still don't know where she is. Of course, I'm calling, hoping you might be able to help."

"I don't know where she is, if that's what you're asking. I haven't talked to her in a couple of weeks."

Charlie thought for a moment. "Would it be all right we got together this morning?"

"I'm still at work," he said.

"You're still working at that gas station, off Weaverville Road?"

"Yes, sir."

"What time you get out?"

There was a pause on the other end. "Not till four."

"You get a break at some point?"

"Yes, sir. Lunchtime."

Charlie turned and looked at Kim. "Jaylen, we'll be out there at noon. We'll try not to disturb your lunch."

"Oh, uh, okay. Sure. You know where it is?"

"Yes I do. I'll see you then."

Charlie hung up the phone and looked at the sheriff. "I hope you don't mind," he said. "I'm not going to lie, hide the fact I've been doing a little digging on my own."

Sheriff Cobb shook his head. "As long as we're all on the same page, and you keep me in the loop, Charlie. My number one concern is seeing to it we get this young lady back safely. Whatever it takes."

Frank said, "You mind telling me who Jaylen is?"

"Haley's boyfriend. Maybe ex, I'm not sure. The father, John Moore, gave me his name. Apparently, she left the house, told the father she was moving in with him."

"With the boyfriend?" Frank said. "Then she ends up living over at the shopping center instead?"

Sheriff Cobb picked up one of the photos and pointed to the blurry face in the picture. "You don't think this is him here, do you?"

Charlie shook his head. "From what I've pieced together so far, just doing a little research this morning,

Jaylen Beard's Native American. His father's Cherokee. I don't believe his mother is, however."

Frank reached for one of the photos, studying the man's face. "Not too many Native Americans I know of with blond hair," he said.

"Some of the other photos we got from Haley's phone, I believe, were of Jaylen." He reached for the phone in front of Sheriff Cobb, tapped the screen, and started flipping through.

"She didn't have a password to get into this?" he said.

Charlie gave Kim a quick look and said to the sheriff, "I did whatever digging I could do on my own. I'm not trying to step on anyone's toes, and of course, no disrespect to Chief Brayden or anyone else, but..."

Sheriff Cobb put up his hand. "You don't have to explain yourself or say another word, Charlie. Chief Brayden will be the first one to admit he let this one slip. But it also doesn't mean they're wiping their hands clean of it all. He's offered whatever resources he can to help. The only difference is the sheriff's office will be the point. All I ask is you keep me abreast. You'll have the same autonomy you always do."

"Oh, don't tell him that," Frank said, letting out a sigh.

The sheriff smiled. He knew Frank wasn't being serious. Charlie had enough of a reputation, not just around western Carolina, but throughout the country. It was no secret he was one of the best, even though Frank sometimes wished he could keep him on a leash.

Sheriff Cobb said, "We need to all do our part, do whatever it takes to find this young lady, pray she's safe, and bring whoever's responsible to justice."

Chapter 11

Charlie and Kim walked across the footbridge from the parking lot at the Fillmore Shopping Center, the air warmer than it had been, the sun shining bright. Both with sunglasses on, Charlie had an envelope in his hand with the photos from Haley's phone, and a few more they pulled from their files.

He saw the man cleaning out the pool, trying to remember what his name was as they got closer. He was almost certain Haley had called him "Steve." He said to Kim, "That's the man I met the first time I came here looking for Haley, when I brought her something to eat." He looked at the photo and approached the man skimming the water inside the fountain, the same thing he was doing the first time Charlie saw him.

"Excuse me," Charlie said.

The man turned and looked at Charlie and Kim. He pulled the skimmer back and rested its pole on the edge of the fountain.

Charlie said, "Remember me?"

"You the marshal?"

Charlie nodded. "This is Deputy Riggins."

The man gave her a quick look but turned back to Charlie. "This about Haley?"

Charlie didn't answer right away. "Your name's Steve, is that right?"

"Yes, sir." He took off his baseball cap and scratched his head. "They know anything yet?" He looked toward the ground, shaking his head. "Still finding it hard to believe. I only wish I could've done something. Been working here five years, never thought I'd see something like this happen.

Charlie opened the clasp on the envelope and pulled out the photos. He had about 10 eight-by-tens and a handful of smaller photos, and held out one of Jessie Redhouse. "You recognize this young man?"

Steve took the photo and looked it over. "Who is he? The one who took her?"

Charlie didn't answer, nodding toward the photo. "Take a real good look. Try and think a little harder if you've ever seen him around." He waited, Steve looking the photo over a little more.

"I think I've seen him around here. Maybe even at some point over the past couple days."

Charlie took the photo of Jessie back and handed him another, this time of Jessie's brother, Dustin. "What about this kid?"

Steve took the photo, rubbing his chin as he looked it over. "I think I've seen him around here too. The two of them, together."

He gave him the photo from Haley's phone. "How about this one? This is likely the man who kidnapped Haley. Whether he was involved with the other two, I just don't know yet. Hoping you can help."

"It's hard to say," Steve said, looking it over. He handed it back to Charlie. "Maybe you have a better photo?"

Charlie held his gaze on the man. "If I did, I wouldn't have shown you this one." He handed the photo back to Steve. "Just give it a good look, all right?"

The man looked up at Charlie, nodding as he took the photo, pulling at his ear as he studied it. "I don't think so," he said.

"I'm going to give you my card," Charlie said, taking the picture back and slipping it into the envelope. He removed a business card from the pocket inside his jacket and handed it to the man. "If you think you see either of these three men around, or if by chance you happen to remember perhaps seeing either one at some point, I'd like you to give me a call." Charlie pointed to one of the numbers on the card. "That there's my cell. Best way to reach me anytime."

Kim said to the man, "Is there anyone else you've seen hanging around more than usual? Especially later, when Haley was around?"

"Well, as I think I told you the other day," he said, nodding at Charlie, "Haley wasn't around much during the day, when I'd be around. She'd take off a little after I'd show up to work, come back later after I'd left."

"How'd you know when she came back, if you were already gone?" Kim said.

Charlie was thinking the same thing.

"Oh, well, I'm just saying. She'd sleep here at night. She had to come back at some point, no?" He grinned. "I appreciate you doing your job, but I hope you're not trying to suggest I—"

"We're not trying to suggest anything," Charlie said. "Just trying to find Haley. Nothing more to it than that." He gave Steve a quick nod. "Like I said, you think of anything else that might help, I'd appreciate the phone call."

Charlie started toward Cabo's Mexican Grille and continued past it toward the side of the building. Kim followed behind, and the two stopped at the dumpster between the walkway around to the back of the building.

"She called me from right here," Charlie said, then turned and looked toward the wooded area, with the parking lot in the distance, through the trees. He walked about twenty feet into it and stopped where he'd found Haley's phone. "I'm still not convinced she dropped it on purpose. That's a lot for a young lady, thinking like that under the circumstances. And considering she'd know the phone was locked..." He kicked the leaves around with his boot. "It was right here, under these leaves."

"I still find it hard to believe you were the first one to see it."

Charlie looked toward the parking lot. "I just don't think the police did what they said they had. I was so pissed, the way they were all just standing around." He headed out from the woods, Kim following, and toward the fountain.

The groundskeeper, or whatever he was called, was nowhere around.

The two continued past the shops on either side of the courtyard area beyond the fountain, toward the parking lot. Music came out over the speakers, although none of the shops looked to be open yet. They walked over the wooden footbridge and out to Kim's Tahoe.

"If nobody from the sheriff's office will be coming over here by the time we get back from talking to Jaylen

Beard, we oughta come back here, show these pictures around."

Kim stepped up and got in on the driver's side as Charlie stood outside the passenger door, looking toward the fountain, until he finally stepped in and closed the door. "What do you say we go visit Jessie and Dustin's aunt? See if there's a chance she's seen them?"

"At the rehab center?"

Charlie nodded. "It's only ten minutes from here. If she's close enough with her nephews to let them stay at her place, then who knows if she's spoken with them?" He tapped the phone's screen with his thumbs, then turned it to Kim.

She typed the address into the GPS on the dashboard.

———

Kim turned the Tahoe into the nursing and rehabilitation center off Reynolds Mountain Boulevard, where Carol Redhouse had been living since suffering a stroke a few months earlier. It was a three-story brick building with a circular driveway and a couple of vans parked at the entrance, both with *Reynold's Mountain Nursing and Rehabilitation* painted on the side.

They walked in through the automatic sliding door, and right away, the odor alone reminded Charlie of going to visit his grandmother when he was a kid, after she, too, suffered a stroke. But she hadn't even been able to speak, and it made him wonder if Carol Redhouse could be in a similar situation. He hadn't really thought about Ms. Redhouse being in a similar predicament. Although, as far as he knew, she wasn't nearly as old as his grandmother was at the time.

It was the smell when they walked through the door that hit Charlie. He whispered to Kim, "No matter how many of these places you walk into, they all have the same awful smell."

Kim gave him a look, like she didn't like the comment. "You should be careful. You might end up here yourself one day."

He shook his head, his voice low as they approached the woman behind the reception desk. "I'd ask you to shoot me dead instead, if you're still talking to me by then."

Kim leaned on the top of the chest-high desk. She had her badge out and showed it to the young woman. "Deputy U.S. Marshal Riggins." She nodded toward Charlie. "This is Deputy Harlow. We're here to talk to Ms. Carol Redhouse."

The woman looked from Kim to Charlie. "Ms. Redhouse is quite popular today," she said, smiling. She turned the clipboard and pointed to the sheet on top. "Please sign here," she said.

"Someone was here to see her?" Charlie said.

The woman behind the desk nodded. "Her nephew just got here a few moments ago."

Charlie started down the hall. "What's the room number?"

"Two-oh-eight," the woman said.

Charlie was at the elevator, pushing the button multiple times, but looked toward the door ten feet away to a sign with a picture of stairs and an arrow. He ran from the elevator and opened the door without looking back for Kim, but she came through the door right behind him.

He ran up the stairs, taking long strides, skipping every other step on his way to the second floor. He yanked open the door and looked right.

A young man stepped onto the same elevator Charlie would have been in, had he only waited another few seconds.

Charlie knew, without a doubt, it was Dustin Redhouse who disappeared out of sight.

Charlie ran down the hall toward him, but it was too late. The doors had already closed. "The stairs!" Charlie yelled, running past Kim to the door he'd just come through. He ran down the stairs and made it to the ground floor in no time, running through the door and into the hall. He turned for the elevator, expecting to see Dustin, but the doors didn't open.

He yelled, "Second floor!" running past her and back to the stairs toward the second floor. "Wait down here."

He ripped open the door and turned right, saw Dustin way down the other end of the hall, running full speed away from him.

"Dustin!" he yelled, thinking for a second about pulling his Glock but thought better of it, moving as fast as he could to catch him.

But Dustin turned into one of the rooms and slammed the door closed. Charlie heard it lock on the other side, stopped, and pounded on it with his fist. "Open the door, Dustin!"

A nurse walked out from another room, her eyes opened wide. "What's going on here?"

He showed his badge. "U.S. Marshals Service," he said, trying to turn the knob. "I need to get in this room!"

The nurse took a key from her pocket and slipped it into the door, opening it right away without another question.

Charlie pushed open the door and saw an old man in bed, eyes closed. A cool breeze came through the room, the curtains blowing away from the window. Charlie hurried across the room, saw the window was wide open with the screen busted out.

He stuck his head through the opening and looked down toward the ground.

Dustin ran across the grass with a bad limp, not moving as fast as he had been in the hall.

Charlie ran out of the room, down the hall and to the stairs, skipping every other step once again. He made it to the ground floor where Kim was standing by the entrance, blocking it.

"He jumped," Charlie said, going past her and out to the parking lot. He ran around to the other side of the building and across the grass to where he saw Dustin. He went as far as the edge of the woods where the green grass ended. "Dustin!" he yelled, running into the woods after him. His breathing was heavy as he tried to ignore the thumping he felt in the back of his head.

He looked back at Kim, running after him. "Get the Tahoe!" he yelled, keeping his hands up in front of him as twigs and branches whipped his face. He could see Dustin up ahead, moving fast enough, Charlie wondered how long he could keep up. But he wasn't about to quit. "Dustin!" he yelled again, as if the kid would stop and wait for him.

Charlie had gone at least half a mile when he finally stopped. He'd lost sight of Dustin but was now surrounded by trees so thick, the sun barely came through. He scanned back and forth, not even sure which direction he should go.

He removed the small handheld compass from his pocket, knowing that heading southeast would get him toward Weaverville Road. Not a short walk. He looked back but realized he was deep in the woods. He wondered if he should walk back in the direction toward the nursing home but instead pulled out his phone and called Kim.

"Where are you?" he said, as soon as she answered.

"Just turned east on North Merrimon," she said. "Any luck?"

"Son of a bitch is fast," he said. "Looked to me he got hurt jumping out that window, but it didn't seem to matter once he got moving."

"Where are you now?" she said.

Charlie looked around. "In the woods, heading southwest. Can't be that far off, I can almost hear the road. But I'm going to keep looking for him; he was running in the same direction, toward the road south of me."

"Should I call Frank?" she said.

"Yeah, might as well. And maybe see if we can get anyone else around who can help. I'll call Sheriff Cobb. I'm sure he'll want to join the fun."

Charlie hung up with Kim and right away dialed the sheriff's cell phone. It rang four times before it was finally answered.

"Sheriff Cobb? It's Deputy Harlow."

"You must've just spoken to Frank?"

"Frank?" Charlie said. "No, not since this morning."

"Oh, uh, okay. He said he was going to call you."

Charlie kept walking and looked at his phone when another call was coming in. "There's Frank right now, calling on the other line. I'll call him back as soon as we're done, but I just wanted you to know I almost had my hands on Dustin Redhouse. He was up visiting his—"

"Sorry to interrupt, Charlie, but this is something you're going to want to hear: We just got a call, a woman's body's been found up Mount Mitchell, behind the gift shop."

Charlie stopped in his tracks. "Is it her?"

"We don't know yet. I'm on my way up there right now."

Chapter 12

Kim picked Charlie up in a Bojangles Chicken parking lot, off North Merrimon Avenue after he finally made it out of the woods, then headed north on Weaverville Road.

"Frank didn't answer, must've been talking to Sheriff Cobb when I called him," she said, her eyes on the road. "Did you talk to him?"

Charlie gripped the leather handle over the passenger door, his right arm hanging. "He's on his way up there now, said the sheriff was debating if he should contact Haley's father, but decided to wait until we got up there." He looked down at his phone and dialed. "I'm calling Jaylen, let him know we'll be swinging by later than planned."

"They don't know if it's her," Kim said. "So let's not even jump to any conclusions just yet."

Charlie nodded as he put the phone up to his ear. After a handful of rings, the call went to voicemail. "He's not answering." He hung up and searched on his phone for Al's Gulf, found the number and called it right away.

A young man answered, "Al's Gulf."

"Is this Jaylen?"

"Jaylen? No, he left."

Charlie said. "Left for *where*?"

"I have no idea. He said he was sick, took off a little over an hour ago."

Charlie glanced at Kim and said, "What time was this?"

The young man on the other end was quiet, pausing a moment. "Who *is* this?"

Charlie didn't answer. "Never mind." He hung up the phone, looking at Kim. "Jaylen Beard left work."

She gave Charlie a quick glance. "That's a little odd, isn't it?"

The two were quiet for at least the next mile.

Charlie picked up his phone and dialed Jaylen's cell phone again. This time he put the phone on speaker, listened to it ring at least five times before the voice-mail greeting came on with Jaylen's voice. Charlie waited for the tone and said, "Jaylen, this is Deputy Marshal Harlow. We've had a change of plans, so we'll need to reschedule for a little later this afternoon. I know you're at work, but do me a favor as soon as you get this and call me back. Same number you called me on before."

He ended the call and placed his phone on top of the dashboard. "Let's see if he calls."

———

Kim turned the Tahoe off of Route 128, into the parking lot, stopping in the No Parking zone next to a row of picnic tables in front of the gift shop on the right. There were three vehicles parked near the red wooden sign with the arrow that said, Mount Mitchell Summit Trail. Two vehicles were from the Yancey County Sheriff's Office, another from Buncombe County. A Burnsville rescue truck was parked up closer toward the wooded area behind the gift shop, where Charlie could see a small crowd of uniformed officials through the trees.

He stepped out of the car and felt a cool breeze, just as a blue Ford F-150 pickup drove up and parked behind them.

Frank stepped out, slipping his arms into his U.S. Marshals jacket, walking toward Charlie and Kim. "You two just got here?"

Charlie said, "Took me a bit of time to get out of those woods. I remember not too long ago I could catch a kid, didn't matter how fast he was."

Frank looked down at Charlie's heavy boots but didn't say anything else.

The three walked together around to the back of the gift shop. Yellow police tape ran along the trees before the land dropped down into the woods.

Frank ducked under the tape first, and Charlie stood still, looking down to where he could see the body, covered, thirty or so feet from where he stood.

Kim gave him a quick glance and went under the tape after Frank, climbing down the rocky slope into the wooded area. She almost slipped on the rocks and soil rolling out from under her but kept her balance. "You coming?" she said, looking back at Charlie.

He watched at first, looking through the short red spruce trees under the shade of the maples and yellow birch blocking all but a few yellow streaks of sunlight. Charlie was pretty good about keeping himself calm in most circumstances, but his heart pounded hard in his chest. He ducked under the tape and made his way down the slope. It was quiet. Or maybe he'd blocked out most of the sound, other than sticks snapping and leaves crunching under his boots, as though it amplified in his head.

Sheriff Cobb turned when Frank walked up behind him. He watched like he was waiting for Charlie and Kim to get closer, until finally shaking his head. "It's not her."

Charlie walked past the sheriff to get a closer look. The sheet had been pulled back, exposing the victim's colorless face when a deputy from Yancey County crouched down, looking her over. She was young, although Charlie thought maybe not as young as Haley. It was hard to tell. He felt guilty for having a brief sense of relief that it wasn't Haley Moore, then let out a sigh and turned away. He gave Kim a look, wondering if there was something she might say.

But neither said a word and started back toward the parking lot.

Frank stood talking to Sheriff Cobb and one of the deputies from the Yancey Sheriff's Office. As Charlie and Kim walked by, he said, "We have no way of knowing this is related or not. So let's not overreact until we—"

"Nobody's overreacting," Charlie said. "But maybe we should assume it is." He continued walking in the direction of the gift shop, back up the rocky terrain and toward the Tahoe.

Frank and Kim both followed.

Frank said, "Sheriff Cobb has his deputies looking for Dustin Redhouse. Got all those woods surrounded right now, so unless he's going to stay in there…"

"I came out the back parking lot of a Bojangles restaurant; nobody even saw me. I didn't see a single deputy down there. At this point, I can almost guarantee he's gotten out of there already. So I'm not sure it matters."

"You're not sure it matters? Don't we still want to find him?" Frank said.

Charlie leaned against the Tahoe's front fender, staring around the side of the gift shop toward the woods. "I'm not sure Dustin or Jessie are guilty of anything, other than knocking a federal marshal in the head with a two-by-four."

Kim said, "But, if they're on the run and hiding out… You don't run if you have nothing to hide."

Charlie felt the area on the back of his head. "Those two boys been running their whole lives. They see a cop or a badge, or any man of the law approaching them, their first *instinct* is to fight or run." He looked from Kim to Frank. "You both saw that photo. It wasn't Jessie or Dustin."

"So then why'd you run after him, if you don't think he's done anything wrong?" Frank said. "Just for fun?"

"I'm not saying they weren't involved. Or that they don't know anything about what happened." He looked toward the wooded area. "I'm not saying they're altar boys."

Frank looked down toward the laid brick area under their feet with a No Parking sign five feet from where they stood. "I know you've heard me say it enough times,

Charlie, but we're not here to decide who is and isn't innocent." He turned and looked toward Sheriff Cobb, coming up over the hill, out of the woods. "If the sheriff wants us to help find the Redhouse brothers; that's what we're going to do."

Charlie looked away from Frank, toward the parking lot where onlookers stood whispering to each other, watching the scene in the woods. He turned to Kim. "No word from intelligence? They must have *something* they can share on that photo by now, no?"

Kim said, "We haven't given them much time." She looked at her phone. "But if you really want me to, I'll call, see where things stand. You know how much they love when we breathe down their necks, like they have nothing else on their plates."

"Go ahead," Frank said to Kim. "Give 'em a call. Tell them I told you to, if they give you any shit."

Sheriff Cobb walked over, shaking his head. "Coroner thinks the young lady may've broken her neck. Appears to have a pretty severe head injury." He looked back over his shoulder toward the woods. "They're going to let me know as soon as they have any information or come across any clues. Hopefully, they find something out here, or by talking to some of the people around." He nodded toward the gift shop. "The sheriff's deputies are inside questioning employees, see if there's anyone that any of 'em might've seen."

Charlie looked toward the front door to the shop. "You already share those photos with Yancey County? The ones we gave you, from Haley Moore's phone?"

Sheriff Cobb chewed the inside of his cheek. "All counties in North Carolina and parts of Tennessee have received the images. That included Yancey."

Charlie said, "What I'm asking is if they're showing that photo to the employees in that shop? Do the deputies asking the questions understand the potential connection between this woman's body and—"

"Why in the hell do you think we got the call up here?" Sheriff Cobb's eyes were narrowed, his eyebrows tight. "You think it was just by coincidence, we all just got invited up here to come catch ourselves a look?"

Frank put his hand on the sheriff's shoulder. "I don't think that's what Charlie's trying to say, or he meant any harm by it, Ross. He's just wondering—and it's a fair enough question—if the employees in that store, or anyone else who those deputies might be talking to, have gotten a chance to take a look at the photo."

Sheriff Cobb cleared his throat and nodded. "I understand, Frank. Let me just get confirmation his department's all on the same page." He turned and started back toward the woods where the Yancey County sheriff was just coming up over the hill.

Charlie opened the door to the Tahoe and reached in for the envelope. He took it out and started for the front door to the gift shop.

"Charlie!" Frank said, "What the hell do you think you're doing?"

But Charlie didn't stop, walking inside the gift shop.

One of the Yancey County deputies was speaking with an older woman wearing a red smock with "Mount Mitchell" and an illustrated mountain printed in white on the front of it.

Charlie stepped in the way, facing the woman. "Excuse me, Deputy," he said. He held the photo. "Ma'am, does this man, by any chance, look familiar to you?"

She looked at Charlie, looked at the deputy like she wasn't sure what had just happened, then took the photo from Charlie. "Who is this?" she said.

"Excuse me," the deputy said, putting his hand on Charlie's shoulder from behind. "We're in the middle of questioning this—"

"Deputy U.S. Marshal Charlie Harlow," he said, turning to show his badge to the deputy. "Just give me a moment, if you don't mind?"

"Well, it's a bit blurry," the woman said, studying the photo. After a good twenty seconds, she looked up at

Charlie. "Does he have anything to do with that poor woman back there?"

Charlie didn't answer. "Do you recognize the face?"

She looked down at the photo. "It's hard to say for sure, but I believe, yes, this young man has been here before." She called for another female employee, much younger but with the same red smock, who was speaking with another deputy. "Cara, does this man look familiar? He's been in here before, hasn't he?" She handed her the photo.

The girl, probably no more than sixteen years old and looking nervous, the way she had her arms crossed in front of her, took the photo and looked it over. She nodded right away, without hesitation. "I've seen him before. He used to walk the trail every once in a while. It's hard to tell, the photo is so blurry.

Charlie looked from the girl to the other woman. "Any chance you saw him today or over the past couple of days?"

Both shook their heads at the same time.

The older woman said, "I think it's been at least a few weeks. There was a time he was here often, maybe in the spring." She tucked her hands into the pockets of her smock. "I believe he drives a pickup truck—one of those smaller ones—and always has tools in the back of it."

"Tools?" Charlie said, eyeballing the deputy standing still, not saying much of anything. "What kind of tools?"

"Tools, like, I don't know... yard tools. Shovels, rakes, that sort of thing."

"You remember the color?"

"Kind of a light brown, beige."

"And when you say 'small,'" Charlie said, "you know what it was? Something like a Chevy S-10? Or..."

"I think it might've been a Nissan." She turned to the other younger woman. "Did you ever see it?"

The girl shook her head without saying a word.

The woman tugged at her ear, playing with one of her earrings. "I'd be outside watering the plants in the mornings; that's the only reason I could tell you what kind of vehicles people who come here might drive. Especially the ones like that young man, who might come here more often to hike the trail."

Charlie looked toward the door and could see Kim through the glass on her phone standing outside, next to Frank, by the passenger-side door of her Tahoe. "Thank you, Deputy," he said, handing him the photo. "You might want to hold on to that. There's a good chance it's the man we want."

Chapter 13

Frank was waiting at the table when Charlie and Kim walked into the office and made a beeline for the conference room. They were expected to be on the call with Ray Morgan, from the Criminal Intelligence Branch.

Frank leaned to reach the phone, set in the middle of the long table. "Charlie and Kim just walked in." He looked at them both as they slid two chairs out from under the other side of the table. "What took you so long?"

"We stopped at Al's Gulf, in Woodfin. Stopped by to see if we could find Haley Moore's boyfriend—ex-boyfriend—but the kid left work earlier in the day, not long after we spoke to him this morning. We swung by on the way back from Mount Mitchell, but nobody knows where he is."

"Nobody?" Frank said. "You go to his home?"

Charlie shook his head and reclined back in the chair. "Sheriff Cobb has his deputies heading over there. I just meant nobody at Al's Gulf, where he works, knows where he is. He's not even answering his phone. But soon as we get out of here, we're heading out to Park Road Bowling. That's the other place he works."

Frank looked a bit perplexed. "Are you telling me nobody else has spoken with this kid yet? You sure about that?"

"I believe somebody from Asheville PD may have, before it was handed over to the sheriff's office. But I can't say for sure. I just figured maybe he could give us some kind of direction, see if the face in that photo rings a bell."

Frank leaned back from the table. "Sorry, Ray. Why don't you go ahead."

"I'd love to," he said. "Now, I just want to be clear. We're still working on this. So far, we've yet to get any kind of a clean match to that photo, but we do have a couple of possibilities we're going to dig a little deeper into. Frank, you have everything I sent you?"

Frank picked up an eight-by-ten print in front of him. "I'm looking at a photo, right in front of me. Yes, Ray. Go ahead."

Ray said, "One is a young man, Kyle Richards—killed a woman when he was just eighteen in Newport Beach,

California. He's twenty-three years old now, been on the run for five years without a single lead in all that time. There's a possibility he's deceased, but it's never been confirmed. Whether or not he, at some point, made his way out to North Carolina is anyone's guess.

Frank slid a photograph across the table. "This is him."

Ray said, "Remember, the photo was taken when he was eighteen, still in high school."

Charlie leaned forward in his chair and opened the envelope with the image of the man from Haley's phone. He compared the two photos, side by side. "I'm not seeing it," he said. "You got something I'm missing here, Ray?"

"Like I said, Charlie, we're still working on it. But we're using facial recognition software that provides us a match. Those photos you sent us weren't exactly what we'd consider clean, but with the technology we have, sometimes it doesn't matter. It'll pick up features in the face we may overlook with the naked eye."

"Well, my naked eye isn't all that bad, and I'm not seeing it, Ray. Looks to me you're grasping at straws here. No disrespect, but..."

The line, and the conference room, went quiet.

Kim leaned in toward Charlie and picked up the photo of Kyle Richards. "What else can you tell us about him, Ray?"

Ray said, "Frank should have everything. I can go over it with you, but... Frank, you have those files I sent over?"

"I have the photos," Frank said. "Was there something else you sent over?"

"I emailed a couple of links, to give you access," Ray said. "Same time as the photo."

Frank pushed his chair out from the table. "Shit, let me take another look. I was in a hurry when I got back. Sorry, Ray. Give me a minute." He walked out from the conference room and into his office.

"While Frank gets that," Charlie said. "You have anyone else you can share?" He stood up and leaned across the table, grabbing another photo from where Frank was sitting. "Who's this in the other photo Frank printed out? Blond-haired kid, looks real young?"

"That's Aaron Jacobs. Been on the run two years now, attempted kidnapping, sexual assault, and armed robbery. He also shot a cop."

"Dead?"

"The officer? No, he survived."

Charlie said, "How old's the kid?"

"Twenty-six."

"Are you kidding me?" Charlie compared the two photos. "And this photo here's only from two years ago? I would've guessed maybe sixteen, and that's pushing it." He looked at Kim, showing her the two photos. "This looks a little more like it, wouldn't you say?"

Kim nodded, laying both photos down on the table. "Same hair, the way it's parted in the middle."

Charlie held up the photo and leaned back in his chair. "Where's he from?"

"Grew up in Fairfax County, Virginia."

"Didn't run very far, only makes it to the next state over." He shook his head. "Are you sure that computer you're using to match these up is working all right?" He tossed the photo across the table. "I don't know, Ray. You send anything else?" He straightened up and looked through the doorway toward Frank's office. "Frank? You find it?"

Frank leaned out the doorway from his office and into the hall, had the phone to his ear, pointing to it.

"Looks like Frank decided to make a phone call," Charlie said. "What can you tell us about... What did you say the first one's name is? The one from California?"

Before Ray could answer, Frank walked into the conference room. "That was Sheriff Cobb on the phone.

Canton Police just picked up Dustin and Jessie Red-house in a stolen van, heading west on Route Forty."

———

Charlie turned the Suburban into a parking space on Main Street and parked in front of the Canton Police station. The air felt cooler, the sky already somewhat dark as he and Kim stepped out.

He opened the glass door on the front of the building and walked in after Kim. There was nobody in the small station's lobby, the chair behind the desk on the back wall empty. "They close for the day?" Charlie said, giving Kim a quick grin.

The inside of the building had a somewhat musty odor like you'd expect in an old building, although it had only been built thirty or so years ago.

A door opened in front of them, to the left of the desk. A uniformed officer, with a cup in one hand and some kind of powdered pastry snack wrapped in plastic in the other, sat behind the desk. He chewed and swallowed whatever he was eating, wiping his mouth with the back of his hand. "Can I help you?"

"U.S. Marshals Service," Charlie said, showing his badge to the officer. "We're here to speak with a couple of your detainees?"

The officer sipped his coffee to wash down what was left in his mouth, nodding. "Oh, right. The two brothers. There's a sheriff and deputy back there already, from Buncombe County." He opened the door he'd just come through. "This way."

Charlie and Kim followed him through the door and down a short hall. They turned into a room no bigger than the inside of Charlie's Winnebago, maybe smaller. Sheriff Cobb sat across a long table from Dustin and Jessie Redhouse. Deputy Mike Carson, who Charlie knew from over the years, had his back to the door but turned when the three walked in.

A Canton officer sat at the table with the sheriff, who introduced him to Charlie and Kim.

Charlie stepped to the table, looking down at Jessie and Dustin Redhouse. "Steal a vehicle, and you're not even smart enough to keep it a little under the speed limit? Makes our job easier, doesn't it?" He looked at Sheriff Cobb.

The sheriff stood up from the table, had a crooked grin on his face. "They claim to know nothing about anything that has to do with Haley Moore," he said.

Charlie saw the photos on the table. "Nothing about anything?" he said, shifting his gaze back to Jessie and Dustin, their hands cuffed behind their backs, hanging their heads, gazes fixed on the table. It was the first time he'd seen Jessie since their run-in at the aunt's house, where Charlie hit him with the same two-by-four piece of wood Jessie used to hit him first. "How's your head, Jessie?"

Jessie didn't answer, but gave Charlie a quick glance out of the corner of his eye.

Charlie turned to Sheriff Cobb. "What about that photo?"

The sheriff shook his head. "Won't say a word about it."

Charlie stepped around Sheriff Cobb and turned the chair the sheriff had been sitting on—sitting on it backward and facing the brothers. He folded his arms on top of the backrest. "If you know anything about Haley Moore, you'd best start talking. It's only going to get harder on you if you don't. I can promise that."

Jessie shook his head. "We don't have nothin' to do with her. We never did."

Charlie glared back at Jessie. "You sure as hell aren't acting like someone who had nothing to do with it." He turned his head and pointed to the back of it, his bandage gone but the stitched-up wound still visible in the middle of the area that had been shaved. "I can see to it you get at least three years for assaulting a federal officer. Throw in the charge for a stolen vehicle, you're looking at another, what, maybe twenty or so months behind bars?"

Dustin still hadn't looked up at Charlie, but Jessie was staring straight at him.

Charlie continued, "You know, I'd be happy to see to it the incident at Coyote Grille brings you another couple of charges. Maybe tack on another twenty-four months, if you'd like. And that goes for you, too, Dustin."

Dustin finally looked up.

"How does that all sound to you boys?" Charlie said.

Neither one responded.

Sheriff Cobb leaned with his hands down on the table. "We have someone who can place you at that shopping center over the past few days. And Deputy Harlow knows you went there after you were blabbing about this poor young lady at the Coyote Grille. But, for some reason, he doesn't seem to believe you're the ones who did the actual kidnapping. I'm not so sure, myself."

"All you two have to do," Charlie said, "is tell us if you know something. If you have some kind of idea who might be responsible, maybe we can get the judge to take it easy on you. I can't make any promises, but..." He glanced at Kim watching him, making promises the way he always did to suspects when he usually had no power at all to make any such deals. "All we're asking is for you to cooperate with us, tell us what you know."

Jessie and Dustin looked at each other, but neither one would talk.

Charlie cleared his throat and stood up from the table. He looked from Kim to Sheriff Cobb, over at Deputy Carson, and the officer. He kept his voice quiet and pulled Sheriff Cobb and the officer off to the side, keeping his back to Jessie and Dustin. "You mind giving me a few minutes alone with these two?" he said.

Kim stepped up to the three. "Charlie, what are you—"

"I just want to have a word with them, alone," he said. "Sometimes, I explain to them a little more about what a U.S. Marshal does, that my only hope is to find Haley. Maybe, you know, I can get them to talk without everyone else in the room."

Sheriff Cobb stared back at Charlie, looking hesitant—as did the officer—both likely unaware of what Charlie might've had in mind.

"Five minutes," Charlie said.

The sheriff and the officer both exchanged a glance and nodded, turning to Charlie.

The officer said, "Five minutes?"

Charlie nodded, his voice in a whisper. "Worth a try, isn't it?"

Sheriff Cobb and his deputy followed the officer out the door.

But Kim didn't leave. "I'm staying right here," she said, crossing her arms.

Charlie put his hand on her back and led her toward the door. "Come on, five minutes, Deputy. Me and the boys just need to have a heart-to-heart." He grinned, his gaze fixed on Kim's as she stood in the hall. "Nothing to worry about." He reached for the door, his hand on the knob.

"Charlie, you can't—"

He closed the door and locked it, turning to the two brothers at the table.

"All right," he said, leaning with his hands down on the other side of the table looking across at the two brothers. "Now, just so you two understand, a U.S. Marshal isn't a police officer. Not like the two out there. It's not my job to investigate a crime or determine who is and who isn't guilty. I don't judge... it's not what we do. However, it is my job to find people. I track down the bad guys. If someone tells me someone's bad, I'll find him." He cleared his throat. "That makes sense to you boys?"

Jessie and Dustin both looked at Charlie, but neither one answered.

"What I'm trying to say is you can tell me anything, without the same implications there might be, were you to, for instance, tell the sheriff or that officer out there. All I ask is that we stop playing games. You help me, as I already told you, I'll do what I can to help you."

Charlie looked to his right toward the door, dragged a chair around to the other side of the table and put his boot up on the chair. He stared at Jessie, waiting for him to look his way.

But Jessie looked straight ahead as if paying Charlie no attention.

Charlie said, "How about we start with one of you telling me how you knew about Haley Moore, and who it was you told after you went there looking for her?"

Dustin, on the other side of Jessie, spoke up right away. "We never went there looking for her. I swear."

Jessie elbowed his younger brother, kept looking straight ahead and acted as if Charlie wasn't there.

"Well, that's not exactly true," Charlie said. "I spoke with Haley, and there's someone else who's sure he saw you there. Haley said there were a couple of young men, seemed to be drinking, staring at her, said these two young men were creeping her out." He grabbed a strand of Jessie's long hair and yanked it, pulling Jessie's head back. "One of 'em just happened to have long hair."

Charlie let go, but as soon as he did, Jessie, handcuffed, knocked his chair back and stood up, went nose to nose with Charlie and stared into his eyes. "We ain't telling you shit."

Charlie grabbed him by the shirt and pushed him back into Dustin, still seated in his chair. "I'm not leaving here until you start talking." He reached for Jessie, pulled him up off his brother, and threw him face-first into the wall.

Jessie dropped to the floor, blood dripping down his face. "You broke my nose!" he yelled.

Charlie grabbed Jessie by the shirt and lifted him to his feet, teeth clenched. "I want you to tell me right now how you knew Haley was sleeping at that shopping center. I know someone told you about her. I heard every word at Coyote Grille... the way you were talking about her like she was a piece of meat."

"Leave him alone," Dustin said, turning in his chair. "We don't know nothin'."

"That's a double negative," Charlie said, holding Jessie still with one hand and reaching for Dustin with the other, ripping him from the chair by the back of the shirt. He dragged Dustin to the table, grabbed the photo, and had Dustin's hair clumped up in his hand, his face pinned with his cheek against the top of the table. Charlie held the photo up to his face. "This is your last chance to tell me who this is."

Dustin wouldn't answer, and Charlie raised his head, grasping his hair, and slammed him down on the table. "Start talking!"

Dustin let out a cry. "Okay, okay," he said, pleading. "It's Travis Crane. I know it is. He has... he has an older brother, works at the shopping center where that girl was sleeping."

"His brother?" Charlie said, turning to look at Jessie getting up to his feet. "Who's his brother? You have a name?"

Jessie said, "It's Steve. He's the maintenance guy over there, cleans out the pool."

Charlie let go of Dustin and looked over the photo. "Did he have anything to do with it? They both kidnapped her?"

Dustin said, "We had nothing to do with it. We don't even know if he has her or not. But that's him in that photo. That's all we know."

Chapter 14

Charlie stopped the Suburban behind Sheriff Cobb's vehicle parked at the top of the driveway. He looked into headlights coming at him and saw the vehicle was from the Asheville PD.

Officer Billy Leader stepped out of the car. "Came as soon as I got your message," Billy said, walking up to Charlie and Kim. "I knew Travis Crane as a kid, but can't tell you the last time I saw him. Last I knew he'd moved out to Tennessee."

Charlie looked toward the ranch house at the bottom of the driveway, as dark around it as it was inside. "Sheriff Cobb has indicated he'd been living here with his brother, Steve."

"This is the house he grew up in," Billy said. "Mrs. Crane passed away about two or three years ago, left the house to Steve."

Deputy Mike Carson stepped out of the passenger seat of Sheriff Cobb's car and walked toward Charlie, Kim, and Billy Leader, standing by the Suburban.

If it were up to Charlie, he'd charge the house and kick in the door, drag Travis and his older brother out by the hair. But it wasn't up to Charlie. Unlike so many other times that he turned to both the sheriff's office and Asheville Police to help track a fugitive, it was the other way around. Sheriff Cobb was in charge. He knew the sheriff preferred a calmer, more methodical approach. And with the election a little more than a month away, the sheriff wasn't likely to bend the rules the way Charlie would.

The sheriff pointed down the driveway. "Charlie, how about you and Deputy Riggins go down around back, make sure nobody tries to slip out when Deputy Carson and I knock on the door, see if we can do this without causing too much of a ruckus.

A ruckus? Charlie thought. *Kick the goddamn door down and rip everyone out of bed. Ask questions later.*

Sheriff Cobb said to Billy Leader, "Billy, you mind staying up here, watching the road? Hopefully our vehicles are enough of a deterrence. You never know what someone'll do."

Charlie and Kim walked through the darkness and overgrown grass to the left of the driveway and past the attached one-car garage. There were no windows on the door, and Charlie wondered if that beige Nissan pickup truck was parked inside it.

The only visible vehicle was a gold Buick Regal in the driveway.

Charlie stopped and looked in one of the garage windows, but it was covered with vinyl blinds on the inside.

"You think they're even here?" Kim said, stopping as she got to the back corner of the house to wait for Charlie. "Both Crane brothers own pickup trucks, and there's only room in that garage for one of them."

"There's only one way we're going to find out," he said, glancing toward the top of the driveway at Billy. The sheriff and Mike Carson were likely just about at the front door.

Charlie felt for his Glock and unstrapped it from the holster, but didn't remove it. He looked toward the woods at the back of the yard and saw a shed tucked under the trees, the moon reflecting off the small window in the side of it. He turned and nodded toward the door at the back of the house. "Watch that door," he said. "I'm gonna take a quick look over here." He continued across the grass and pulled on the shed's double doors, trying to turn the knob, but it was locked. He looked in through the window, but it was covered with cardboard inside.

A gunshot rang through the air, and with the quick flash of light, Charlie saw someone in the woods. He ducked behind the shed and could hear the sticks snapping off in the distance until it went quiet. He turned the flashlight toward Deputy Riggins and saw she was lying on the ground. "Kim!" He ran toward her.

"My leg," she said, grasping it, Charlie shining the light on her.

The blood had soaked through her pants.

Charlie pulled a knife from his back pocket and cut through them, exposing the wound, then pulled his shirt off his back and sliced into it with the knife. He tore off a long strip of material and tied it around her bare leg. He had to slow the bleeding.

Charlie reached for his two-way and did his best to sound calm in front of Kim: "Deputy Riggins has been shot. Officer down. We're going to need a paramedic." He gave the address and squeezed Kim's hand, looking into her eyes.

The sheriff and deputy came running around from the front of the house, flashlights out with the beams bouncing around the yard and into the woods. They darted toward Charlie and Kim.

"She was hit," Charlie said, crouching down next to her. "She'll be all right," he said. "Hang in there."

"I'm fine," she said, the strained sound of pain in her voice. "Go get the son of a bitch."

Charlie nodded and looked up at Sheriff Cobb. "Keep an eye on her." He jumped to his feet and took off into the woods without another word.

"Deputy!" the sheriff yelled, but Charlie just kept running straight in the direction he saw the flash from the gun when it was fired. But he only made it in another fifty or so yards when he heard another gunshot and the roar of a car's engine.

Three more shots were fired, followed by an explosive crash. He looked to the front of the house and up the driveway. Billy was in the street, taking another shot at a vehicle with lights off, driving away from him, tires squealing as it disappeared down the road.

The sheriff's vehicle was turned around and across the street, the driver's side crushed like a tin can.

Charlie ran out from the woods and up the driveway and watched Billy take off in his vehicle, speeding down the road, blue lights flashing, until he disappeared around the corner.

Standing at the top of the driveway, Charlie looked back at the house. When he saw that the front door was wide open, he ran inside, going from room to room, flipping on every light switch he could find, kicking in every door. But the place appeared to be empty.

He could smell cigarette smoke and bacon as he walked into the kitchen. A pan on the stove had thick white grease spread on the bottom of it, an open bag of Wonder Bread next to it on the counter, with half the slices on the floor.

A cigarette burned in the ashtray, and Charlie dumped the whole thing in the sink, running the faucet over it.

He opened the back door and looked outside, toward Kim. "She all right?"

Sheriff Cobb was kneeling next to her, doing something with her leg, and asked her how she was doing.

Charlie couldn't hear Kim's answer, but the sheriff yelled back to him: "She says she's all right." He looked back at Charlie. "What the hell happened out front?"

"Someone crashed through your vehicle," he said, walking down the steps. "Billy went after him." He went over to check on Kim. "Where's the damn paramedics?"

Deputy Carson said, "They're on their way."

Charlie kneeled with one knee on the concrete and put his hand on Kim's shoulder. "You hangin' in there?"

She looked at him, her eyes appearing heavy, like she wanted to close them. "It hurts."

"That's a hell of a lot of blood," the sheriff said.

Charlie gave him a look, wanting to say, *With all due respect, Sheriff, please shut your mouth.*

But he didn't. "You'll be all right," he said, hesitant to leave her side.

"I'm fine, Charlie. "Go see what you can come up with. But be careful."

He stood up and went back in the house, through the kitchen, and into the garage. He flipped on the light, and there it was: the old beige Nissan truck, but with the bed empty of the garden tools. He wondered what they could've been for. Maybe the kid was doing landscaping. Or maybe he used them to dispose of a body or two. Although, the way he'd left that poor woman up on Mount Mitchell, he didn't seem to be too worried about leaving a victim out in the open.

Deputy Carson walked in behind Charlie. "There it is," he said, shaking his head. "We had him."

Charlie didn't want to tell him *No you didn't*. If he'd done it his way, he'd have a shotgun at the suspect's head before he even opened his eyes, catch him in a deep sleep he'd wake from with the cold metal against his skin. "What the hell happened?" he said, walking past him and back into the house. He looked at the front door, practically hanging off the hinges.

"We heard the gunshots; both Sheriff Cobb and I ran around back to make sure you both were all right. I guess one of us probably should've stayed out front, but they must've taken the opportunity to clear out."

Charlie started down the hall, the deputy following. "Well, whichever one of 'em was in the woods knew it'd cause enough commotion, give the other a chance to clear out of there." He turned into the first bedroom he saw and went right for the mattress. He lifted the sheets and had a strong feeling someone had recently slept on it, not to mention the body odor hanging in the air. He stepped out of the room and turned into another across the hall. "So you never got a look at anyone?"

Sirens could be heard in the distance.

Deputy Carson stood in the bedroom's doorway. "The shots come from inside the house?"

"The woods," Charlie said, looking around the room, just as empty as the other. It hit him right then he hadn't looked in the shed as he'd intended, before the gun was fired. He walked down the hall, through the kitchen and out the back door.

Red flashing lights reflected off the trees.

Charlie crouched next to Kim. "You doing all right?" He glanced at the blood puddled under her leg on the concrete, the floodlight on the back of the house reflecting off it.

She turned her head, looking toward the woods along the side of the house. "They get away?"

Charlie grinned, put his hand on her shoulder. "Don't you worry about anything else. Paramedics are here." He looked up as a man and woman came around the corner, the bright light from their truck in the driveway lighting up half the yard.

Charlie stood up to get out of their way. "She was shot in the leg." He stepped back as the two paramedics crouched next to her, then turned and walked to the shed.

The barnlike door had a lock on it. Charlie stepped back and raised his boot, trying to knock it off with his heel. But it didn't budge. He looked around on the ground for something he could use, shining the flashlight along the grass and into the leaf-covered woods. A large rock at the back of the shed looked large enough to do some damage. He tucked his flashlight in his belt and picked up the boulder with both hands and carried it to the shed's door. He strained to lift it up high, almost over his head, and dropped it down hard on the lock.

The wood cracked and the handle on the door busted off.

Charlie took out his flashlight and was careful pulling open the door. He raised the light to see what was inside and first saw a blanket and a pillow on the floor. Next to the pillow was a large glass jar half filled with what looked like water. There was a small flashlight leaning up against the shed's interior wall. He turned and looked around the small space and at yard tools, leaning in the corner by the door.

Deputy Carson poked his head inside, looking at the floor. "Someone sleeping in here?"

"At some point," Charlie said. He reached down to lift the blanket, and a book fell out from within, and onto the floor. He grabbed it and looked at the cover. "Marie Force," he said.

"*Who?*"

Charlie showed him the cover. "Marie Force. She's a romance author." He flipped through the pages. "This book belongs to Haley Moore."

Chapter 15

THE SUN WAS BARELY up when Charlie walked out of Mission Hospital at the same time Frank was stepping out from his car and heading toward the entrance.

"Is she all right?" Frank said, the two stopping halfway in the quiet, almost empty, parking lot.

"She's out of surgery, so I'm not sure you can see her just yet. I'm heading back out, keep searching like everyone else."

Frank looked him over. "You look like shit. When was the last time you slept?"

Charlie took off his cap, with the U.S. Marshals emblem stitched on the front, and brushed his hair to the side with his hand. "I'm not even sure."

"Then why don't you go get some rest? Between the sheriff's office and Asheville PD, they've got people out there. You're not going to be of any use the way you are, running on fumes like this."

"I've got a few more hours in me. And it's likely the two are split up. Who knows what they've done with Haley, whether or not she's with one of 'em, or…" He turned and looked toward the hospital's entrance. "I've only been here about an hour, but they were spreading out. It's anyone's guess where they could be right now."

Frank said, "You hear Billy Leader was in an accident? Got T-boned on Route Sixty-Four, crossing into Edneyville. That's the last anyone's seen that Buick he was after."

Charlie said, "Is he all right?"

"Yeah, he's okay. Car's not."

"All the more reason I gotta get out there," Charlie said. "Nobody even knows if the two are still split up or not. I'm guessing there was no chance for whichever one was in the car to pick up the other, not with Billy in pursuit. I figured whichever one was in the woods got left behind, but we spent the whole night searching in there and all around the house, no luck at all. Only reason I left was to get over here, make sure Riggins was all right."

Frank said, "Charlie, we've another little issue on our hands we're going to need to talk about."

"Uh-oh," he said. "I know that look." He put up his hands. "I've been a good boy, doing whatever the sheriff asks."

Frank said, "I don't think he asked you to knock around the Redhouse brothers the way you did out in Canton. You broke the older one's nose, and the younger one claims he's got a concussion, saying you knocked his head into the table."

"Sheriff Cobb told you all that?" Charlie said, knowing Frank never liked the way Charlie took things into his own hands. But it was usually effective.

"I talked to him about it; he's not the one making a big deal of it. But somehow word got out, and the fingers are being pointed at his office. With the election coming up and all, he doesn't want something like this to get in the way of—"

"Are you shitting me?" Charlie said. "That's all he's worried about? His reelection?"

Frank shook his head. "You know how these things are nowadays, Charlie. It all spreads like wildfire, every little thing that happens. The fact the only thing anyone's got on those Redhouse brothers, right now, is stealing a van, they were lucky they made it as far as they did. They won't even get thirty days, if that."

"They were withholding information, Frank. And if I didn't do what I did, they weren't going to say a word about knowing who Travis Crane was. The sheriff's tactics weren't cutting it. I'm sorry, but I did what I had to do."

"I get that," Frank said. "But the word out there is it was someone from the sheriff's office who showed up in Canton and busted the nose of a suspect with his hands cuffed behind his back."

"The *sheriff's* office?"

"That's what I'm saying, Charlie. Somehow word spread that it was the sheriff or someone from his office."

Charlie shrugged. "So, go ahead, tell them it was me."

"Tell who? It's not the news media, Charlie. You know how it is now. Someone got wind of what happened, next thing you know there's photos online of Jessie Redhouse and his busted nose."

"So, what do you want me to do? We've gotten where we are now because of it. Who gives a shit what these clowns have to say, sitting in their underwear in their parents' basement, tweeting out shit about some loser's broken nose?"

"It's just not that easy anymore, Charlie. And I don't want you to get the wrong idea. Sheriff Cobb didn't want to make a big deal out of it, but he's a little concerned where it could go."

"So he's afraid of how it'll look in the papers?" Charlie said.

"Like I said, I wish the newspaper was all we had to worry about."

"This social media bullshit, you wonder why nobody wants to be in law enforcement anymore. Even if you think you try to do the right thing, they want to hang someone. They don't care who it is half the time. I mean, I'm not saying there aren't some issues—and I'm no saint—but I busted this kid's nose and got him to talk. What's the big deal?"

Frank said, "There's just a lot of scrutiny coming our way right now, all right? I don't even mean to be crawling up your ass about it, Charlie. If it weren't for you, we wouldn't have the slightest clue where Haley Moore's been. But I need you to just be considerate of the sheriff right now. Especially when he's the one running the show."

Charlie nodded, fixing his cap on his head as he turned and glanced over at his Suburban.

Frank said, "Why don't you go get yourself a couple hours sleep," Frank said. "I'll let you know how Kim's doing, and then you can get back out there. The sheriff knows he needs us. He knows he needs *you*. But he doesn't need a goddamn zombie out there."

Charlie's phone rang, and he almost rolled off the bed, in such a deep sleep that he didn't know he was inside his Winnebago. He reached for the phone, squinting his eyes with the way the sun blasted through the small window over the bed.

He looked at the screen and saw it was Jennie. He hadn't spoken to her in a couple of days. Ever since their divorce he felt like they talked more than when they were married, although lately, it had been less.

He cleared his throat. "Hello?"

"Charlie? Can you talk?"

"Can I talk?" He sat up on the edge of the bed. "I can talk."

"Are you all right? You sound like you're half asleep."

"I am." He looked at his phone for the time. "Oh shit," he said. "It's late."

"Were you really asleep? I don't ever remember you sleeping till ten."

"I went to bed at seven," he said. "This morning."

"Is everything okay? I just saw on Facebook they arrested a man who works at the Fillmore Shopping Center. You told me about that girl, and—"

"They arrested him?" Charlie jumped up from the bed. "How the... where'd you hear this?"

"I just told you. Facebook."

He hurried around inside, grabbing his watch from the shelf, along with his wallet and badge. His Glock was under his pillow, his holster hung on the knob of the bathroom door. "Who posted it? The sheriff's office?"

"I don't think so. A friend of mine shared it, but it wasn't anyone in law enforcement. Someone shot the video, from a parking lot."

Charlie hadn't even taken off his clothes before he got in the bed a few hours earlier to take what, at the time, was supposed to be a quick nap. He reached for his boots and pulled them on, looking at the screen on his phone to see if he'd missed a call. "I gotta call you back, Jennie." He hung up without another word and tapped the number for Sheriff Cobb's phone. But it rang five times and went to voicemail.

Charlie hung up and called Frank.

It was two rings before Frank answered. "I was just going to call you," he said. "Did you get some sleep?"

Charlie didn't even answer. "Did you know about Steve Crane?"

Frank said, "I know they may've had a sighting out in Fletcher, but—"

"Jennie just called, said he'd been arrested behind a gas station on Cane Creek Road."

"Jennie? How the hell would she know *that*?"

"Someone posted it online. On Facebook. A video."

"Jesus Christ," Frank said. "You talk to anyone else? Sheriff Cobb? He didn't call you?"

Charlie slipped his belt on, looped it through his holster and tucked the Glock inside. "No, he didn't. I called him right before you, but he didn't answer."

"Where are you right now?" Frank said.

"At my place. I'm heading out now."

"You know which gas station?"

"How many can there be on Cane Creek Road? I'll look for the one with all the police vehicles." He was about to hang up. "Oh, Frank? What about Kim? She all right?"

"She'll go home tomorrow. She was asking for you."

———

Charlie had just taken the turn for the ramp onto I-40 toward Asheville when his phone rang. He didn't bother to look to see who it was. "Deputy Harlow."

"Charlie? It's Ross."

"Sheriff, I've been trying to catch you. I've heard through the grapevine you've got Steve Crane in custody?"

"We do. I'm sorry I didn't call you sooner, Charlie. I meant to, it's just—"

"You don't want me messing with your reelection campaign?" Charlie said. "Is that what the problem is?"

"Whoa, now, Charlie. What would make you come out with some kind of BS like that?"

"I'm just asking. I understand you weren't happy with my methods which, in case you chose to ignore the facts, have gotten us a few steps closer to finding a missing young woman and her captors."

"Don't go listening to what other people are saying. I think you know me well enough, Charlie, that I'd tell you right to your face if I had a problem with the way you do things. I know we don't always see eye to eye, and I prefer a somewhat more civil approach to law enforcement than you might, but it doesn't mean I don't appreciate the things you've done, not just in this case, but the dozen or so since I've been sheriff. I know local law enforcement isn't always the priority of the U.S. Marshals Service, but you've always been there when I've needed you."

"Okay," Charlie said. "I appreciate hearing that. But I still don't understand why I had to hear it from my wife, who saw it on Facebook, that Steve Crane had been taken into custody by your office."

"Because it's not Steve Crane," the sheriff said. "We have a man driving a gold Buick with the front end smashed up, said he found it parked off Emmas Grove Road in Fletcher, right before the middle school."

"You shittin' me?" Charlie said.

"Keys were in it."

Chapter 16

Charlie turned into Al's Gulf, the gas station up in Woodfin, and parked the Suburban around the side. He walked around to the front and opened the glass door, the bell over it ringing as he stepped inside.

"Welcome to Al's," the young man said, standing behind the counter.

"You Jaylen?" Charlie said, knowing it was him by the photos he'd already dug up online.

The young man paused, looking around like he was getting ready to dart out of the place.

"I'm going to assume your silence is a yes," Charlie said. "And don't go trying to run off. I'm not in the mood. And I'll get in trouble if I have to shoot you."

Jaylen swallowed, nodding. "You the marshal?"

Charlie showed his badge. "Deputy Marshal Charlie Harlow." He walked to the counter, off to the side, where a pot of coffee looked like it had just been brewed. He grabbed a tall paper to-go cup and filled it to the top, walked it over to the counter and placed it in front of Jaylen. "How much?"

"It's... it's on the house."

Jaylen looked nervous, his eyes still darting around like he wasn't sure what to do.

"You mind telling me why you took off from work yesterday?" Charlie said. "We were supposed to meet. Remember?"

"I'm sorry, I was sick. Some kind of flu or something."

Charlie gave him a quick grin. "Oh. I hope you're feeling better?" He sipped the coffee, made a face from the bitterness. "Ah. Gas-station coffee." It wasn't that he was a coffee snob. Far from it. But being married to Jennie, she'd buy the whole beans and grind them fresh. It made it hard to go back to the only kind of coffee he ever drank until he married her.

Jaylen nodded, swallowed hard again, and looked down at the Glock Charlie had holstered.

The way Charlie held his jacket out of the way, one hand on his hip, he made *sure* Jaylen could see his gun. "The police or anyone from the sheriff's already talk to you about Haley Moore?"

"Both," Jaylen said. "Two different times. Asked the same kind of questions."

"Oh yeah? Like what?"

Jaylen shrugged. "I don't know. If I knew where she was. Asked when was the last time I saw her... why we broke up and whether or not we were still talking."

"Okay," Charlie said. "So, if you don't mind, I'm going to ask you some questions myself. And I've got a good nose for bullshit, so I'd appreciate it if you'd be straight with me."

"I didn't have nothing to do with her disappearing the way she did. I swear, I—"

"I know you didn't. But from what I've been told, just a little while ago, you know Travis Crane. In fact, I understand he was somewhat a friend of yours?"

Jaylen took a moment before he nodded. "When we were younger, we were friends. But that was back in middle school. Maybe a little into high school, but—"

"Are you aware he's the main suspect in Haley's kidnapping?"

Jaylen's eyes went wide. "Travis Crane? You think he kidnapped Haley?"

"He's wanted for not only her kidnapping, but for another woman's murder."

"But... but he was... Travis was a nice kid. Why would he—"

"He was a nice kid, *when*? When you knew him in middle school? Or did you still see him around? I know you and Travis went to school together, grew up in the same town. I imagine you've at least bumped into him now and again, no?"

Jaylen shrugged and nodded at the same time. "I guess so."

"He knew Haley?"

Jaylen looked out the window behind him, toward the gas pumps. An older man with a cane was walking toward the door.

"I have a customer," Jaylen said to Charlie.

The door opened and the bell over it dinged. The old man walked up to the counter, gave Charlie a nod, and placed a ten-dollar bill in front of Jaylen. "Ten. Pump three." He walked out without another word, the bell ringing twice as he opened the door and let it close.

"He's met her once or twice, but I think it's been a while. Honestly, I didn't even know he was still living around here. Last I'd heard, he'd moved away to be closer to this girl he was dating."

"Oh yeah?" Charlie said. "You know her name?"

Jaylen shook his head. "She lives out in Cherokee, or somewhere within the Qualla Boundary."

"She Cherokee?"

Jaylen nodded. "But that was a long time ago." He cleared his throat. "Are you going to find her? Haley?"

"I'm trying," Charlie said. "I'd like to think so. But we need whatever help we can get. So whatever else you can tell me would be appreciated. Maybe start by telling me what happened with you and Haley?"

"What happened? You mean, why'd we break up?"

Charlie picked up his coffee from the counter and took a sip. It had cooled off a bit and he'd gotten somewhat used to the bitterness. "Haley's dad told me she was supposed to move in with you. But that never happened? Is that why she ended up sleeping out at the shopping center?"

Jaylen ripped open a carton of Newport cigarettes and started to stick the individual packs into the slots behind him. He had his back to Charlie but looked at him over his shoulder. "She wanted to move in with me, but I never said I wanted to. She just assumed she could. She hated living with her dad."

"So why didn't you want her to move in with you?"

I moved back home. I had an apartment, but I couldn't afford it. And Haley had gotten fired from her job at the grocery store."

"*Fired?* For what?"

"She got caught stealing books, that's all."

Charlie thought about the novel he found in the shed. "So where do you live now? With your mother?"

"In an apartment, out in Alexander. She lost the house in Asheville, after my dad died."

"Oh, I'm sorry to hear that," Charlie said. "Now, just a couple more things: is there any chance Haley would've known this kid Travis? I mean, enough to maybe go with him?"

"Go with him?" Jaylen said, looking confused. "You mean, would she go somewhere without being forced to?" He finished putting the cigarette packs in the slots behind him and turned, looking down toward the counter. "I'm not sure she knew him well enough to even recognize him, if that's what you're asking. If she did remember him, I think she'd know enough to stay away from him. He was all right when he was younger, but he started hanging around with these two brothers..."

"What two brothers?"

"They live around here now, names're Jessie and Dustin."

"The Redhouse brothers?"

Jaylen looked surprised, nodding. "You know them?"

"Yeah, I know them." But Charlie didn't go into the details, touching the back of his head where the shaved hair around his wound had started to grow. "Anything you want to tell me about them?"

Jaylen shook his head. "I know they're half Cherokee. And they've been in a lot of trouble. But I don't know if that's how Travis met his girlfriend, or—"

"You know her name?"

Jaylen was still, like he was thinking. "I think her name's Yona. I only met her once."

Charlie's phone rang and he looked at the screen. "Excuse me, Jaylen." He answered as soon as he saw it was Kim.

"Hey," he said, walking toward the back of the store. "How're you doing?"

"I'm okay," she said.

"Does it hurt?"

"A little. I have a crack in my shin. The doctor said it'll heal in a couple of weeks as long as I don't do anything too crazy."

"That's not bad," Charlie said, trying to make light of it. "I'm up in Woodfin, talking to Jaylen Beard. And I was just thinking..." He looked over at Jaylen watching him but looking away when Charlie's eyes met his.

"Guess he's not sick?" she said.

"Looks pretty healthy to me," he said. "How about I take a ride over, see how you're doing. I'll fill you in on where things stand. I know you're going to be out of commission for a while, but—"

"Why would I be out of commission?"

"Well, you just said you need a couple of weeks, and—"

"They told me it'd be less than two weeks before it's fully healed. They didn't say I'd be stuck in bed the whole time. I'm fine. Should be out of here by the end of the day."

"Frank said tomorrow morning."

"Sometimes Frank thinks he's my father," she said. "I'm pushing for sometime this afternoon, if the doctor will agree to it."

Charlie smiled. "If you say so." He started toward the front of the store and said to Kim, "You need me to bring you anything?"

"Whoever shot me, his head on a platter." She said it with a slight laugh, but then the phone went quiet for a moment. "Any updates on Haley?"

"Nothing yet," Charlie said, thinking. "I'll see you soon. All right?" He tucked the phone in his pocket and picked up his coffee, reaching into his inside jacket pocket for a business card, which he dropped on the counter. "You hear anything at all, Jaylen, I want you to call me right away. You know of anyone else who might know where Travis Kelly's gone or any word about where Haley could be, I want you to call me. I don't care what time it is. Call me." He raised the to-go cup. "Appreciate the coffee."

Chapter 17

CHARLIE SMILED WHEN HE walked in the hospital room and saw Kim seated in the padded chair in the far corner by the window, clicking through the TV channels with the remote. She had a black boot on her leg propped up on an ottoman.

"You look better," he said. He looked at her leg, the black boot like a ski boot but strapped around her leg all the way up to just below her knee. "How long do you have to wear that thing?"

"Hopefully just a week or two. Cracked my tibia, where the bullet grazed the bone."

"I guess you'll be doing office duty for a few weeks, huh?"

Kim shook her head. "I can walk with it," she said. "We'll just have to see if I can run."

"I don't think that's a good idea," Charlie said.

"Well, I'm not going to sit around that office all day?"

"You can still help without being out in the field. You're going to need to be realistic."

"I am being realistic. I'm fine. I'm not even sure I need it." She leaned forward and ran her hands over her leg. "When I was a little girl, I broke my arm. I cut the cast off myself, it was so damn itchy."

Charlie sat on the edge of the bed thinking about when he was shot in the leg in Afghanistan, and how he took the boot off after a few days. He knew it probably wouldn't have still caused him pain every once in a while if he'd listened to the doctors and left it on a few more weeks. "I'm heading out to Cherokee after I leave here, going to talk to Cody Walker. Jaylen told me Travis Crane has, or had, a girlfriend out there."

"On the Qualla?"

Charlie nodded. "But he doesn't know if they're still together or not. I'm just hoping maybe she'll know something about him, assuming she'd be willing to talk to me."

"Did he say anything else?"

"He also knows the Redhouse brothers and mentioned, being that they're half Cherokee, he thinks Travis met the girlfriend through them. He said Travis was a normal kid until he started hanging around with the brothers."

Kim said, "What's the girl's name?"

"Yona. That's all he could tell me. Didn't seem to know much about her, but I'm hoping Cody will." Charlie looked at his watch. "You mind I take off, head out there now? I told Sheriff Cobb I'd go out there right away, see what I can find."

"He's not going?"

"Sheriff Cobb?" Charlie shook his head. "You know how Cody is. Told the sheriff I didn't think he'd want a bunch of outside law enforcement officials poking around."

Kim nodded, like she understood. "Are you coming back?"

"I'm going to try. You need a ride?"

"I might. But I can call—"

Charlie said, "I'll check with the desk out there, see if they have a better idea of when you'll be released. Either way, I'll be back in a few hours." He walked over to her and placed his hand on her shoulder. "You sure you shouldn't be in bed, getting some rest?"

"I'm fine," she said. "One of the nurses said I could be released closer to the end of the day, once the doctor shows up this afternoon. So don't rush back on my account."

"All right. But if they let you out sooner, give me a call."

"I doubt they will," she said, watching Charlie start for the door. "Charlie? You didn't finish telling me about the brothers."

Charlie turned, looking at Kim leaning, looking over at him.

She said, "Jessie and Dustin. Have you talked to them?"

"Not since I busted Jessie's nose. Frank thought it'd be best if I let the sheriff deal with them. I'm assuming you heard some people are a little upset with the way I handled it?"

Chief of Cherokee Indian Police Cody Walker was outside the station with the hatch of his vehicle, a Ford Explorer, with "Cherokee" painted along the side, wide open. He lifted plastic milk crates out from inside it, placing them on the ground by his feet.

Charlie walked up behind him. "Good afternoon, Chief."

Cody was a big man, both wide and tall without much of a neck coming out from his black, long-sleeved uniform. *Chief Cody Walker* was stitched in gold over his right breast pocket, the gold badge stitched over the left. He smiled, placing a crate down on the ground and reaching out his hand as he straightened up. "Deputy Harlow," he said. "How are you doing, Charlie?"

They shook hands, both with a bearlike grip.

"You get my message?" Charlie said, a feeling Cody did not, with the way he looked back at him.

Cody said, "You called the cell?" He pulled out his phone and looked at the screen. "Oh, there it is. I must have twenty messages on here, just from this morning." He pointed to the crates. "You see what I'm dealing with?"

Charlie looked down and saw the large ziplock bags filled with smaller bags and brick-shaped packages. "Looks like a little of everything?"

"We broke up a fight outside the casino, in the parking lot. Turns out one of the couples involved had stolen plates on their car. We search the car, found all these crates in the trunk." He pointed at the crates. "Meth, heroine, syringes, marijuana, cocaine..."

Two uniformed officers came out from the front door of the station and toward Cody, each one leaning over to pick up a crate. They turned and walked with them back into the station.

"It doesn't end," Cody said.

"No help from the feds?" Charlie said.

Cody cracked a somewhat crooked smile. "This is nothing. FBI came through two months ago, part of a forty-person bust from here to Wisconsin. As soon as you think you have it off the streets, someone else comes in and replaces it." He closed the hatch on his vehicle and picked up one of the two crates. "You mind?" He nodded toward the last one. "If I leave it out here, it'll be gone before I get back."

Charlie picked up the crate and followed Cody up the steps and inside the station.

The building was a small ranch-like structure with a stone exterior, the inside no bigger than a home with a living room and a few rooms down the hall. Four wooden desks took up the immediate area.

Cody walked through an open door and placed the crate down on the floor.

Charlie handed him the crate he was carrying, wiped his hands on his pants, and followed Cody from the room and down a hall to the opposite end of the station.

"So, should I listen to your message, or are you going to tell me why you drove all the way out here without even making sure I was here?" He sat behind his wooden desk. "You're not in trouble again, are you?"

Charlie grinned, tight-lipped, shaking his head. "I'm not. You heard about the young woman abducted out in Asheville."

Cody nodded. "Yeah, of course. The U.S. Marshals involved in that?"

"We're assisting the sheriff's office."

"We've offered to help," Cody said. "Of course, got our eyes open around here, but we are aware there are a couple of suspects that are wanted."

"One of them may have been involved with a girl who lives out here."

"Cherokee?"

Charlie nodded. "Name's Yona. I don't have a last name. I've only gotten the information within the past few hours. So, I'm hoping you might be able to help."

"Yona Cooper?" he said. "We have a few Yonas out here, but they're all older. How old is she?"

"I'd have to guess either late teens or early twenties."

Cody nodded. "Then it must be Yona Cooper. Do you want me to take you out to talk to her? Her father is not someone who would allow her to date a white boy, but you can talk to her. She works at JD's Diner." He got up from his desk. "Yona is a good kid. I would hate to think she'd be involved with a man wanted for kidnapping."

"It's what I've been told, but I'd at least like to talk to her. Anything we can do to get closer to tracking him down. I'd hate to think what'll happen if we don't find him."

Cody said, "There are two brothers; is that correct?"

"Travis and Steve Crane."

Cody walked ahead of Charlie out the door. "So who gave you Yona's name?"

"Actually, the missing girl Haley Moore's ex-boyfriend. In fact, Jessie and Dustin Redhouse were the ones who first gave me Travis Crane's name."

"I haven't heard either of those names mentioned in a while." He stopped and turned to Charlie. "They wrapped up in this somehow?"

"I don't know. They're denying they had anything to do with it, but Jessie Redhouse is the one who led us in the direction of Travis Crane. Of course, he didn't want to do any talking until I had a chance to sit down with him." Charlie grinned.

Cody waved his hand through the air. "I'm glad I don't have to deal with them anymore. They're someone else's problem now."

The two walked past the empty desks and out the front entrance into the parking lot.

Cody opened the driver's-side door to his Explorer. "Get in. I'll drive you out to see Yona."

Chapter 18

CHIEF WALKER PARKED BY the front door at DJ's Diner, a place Charlie had only eaten at once before, but it had been a while. The small parking lot was full, the smell of burgers being cooked coming out in the smoke blowing up from the stack on the roof.

"It looks busy," Charlie said, stepping out from Cody's vehicle.

Cody said, "I'd say come back later, but you should at least check and see if she's here, grab something to eat. And I'm sure you don't want to hang around Cherokee all day."

"I'll do whatever I have to if it'll lead me to Haley Moore."

They walked inside, and Cody nodded toward a young woman who looked to be no more than maybe eighteen, rushing from around the other side of the counter with a tray full of sodas. "That's her," he said.

A woman stepped up behind them. "Good afternoon, Chief. Are you going to sit at the counter?"

Cody shook his head. "We'd like to sit in Yona's section, if that's all right?"

The woman looked surprised and somewhat confused by the request. "Is everything all right?"

Cody smiled. "Perfectly fine," he said, without telling her much of anything else.

She pointed toward the far end of the diner, at a table without anybody seated at it, but there were dirty dishes all over it. "I'll have that table cleaned off right away. Just give me a moment." She walked through the swinging door behind the counter, disappeared into the kitchen, then came back through a moment later behind a young man carrying a rectangular bucket for the dirty dishes, and headed toward the table.

The woman walked back over to Charlie and Cody. "One moment, Chief."

"Must be nice to be looked up to and respected around here," Charlie said. "I've been a deputy marshal eight years, never had anyone move like that to have a table cleared off for me."

"Don't kid yourself, Charlie. Not everyone respects me. Don't forget, I'm an appointed official. They can take the title away a lot faster than they gave it to me." He nodded toward the table in the back corner. "Looks like it's all set." He gestured for Charlie to walk ahead of him.

The woman walked over and handed them two menus. "I'll tell Yona to come right over."

Charlie sat down across from Cody and looked over at Yona, taking the order from another table. She looked young, like a kid, but the closer he looked, the more it looked like there was a chance she could be pregnant. He leaned in toward Cody and whispered, "Is that a baby bump, or does Yona like to drink too much beer?"

Cody glanced over his shoulder at her and turned back to Charlie. He looked surprised. "I don't know. So many pregnancies among our adolescents. Four out of every ten kids, Charlie. And then they wonder why they end up in poverty."

Charlie watched Yona but tried not to stare. He looked away when she started walking toward them.

"Hello, Chief," she said, a bright smile on her face.

She was pretty, with long, straight dark hair and big brown eyes.

"How are you doing, Yona?" Cody said. "And how are your parents doing?"

She nodded, placing her hand on her belly but not saying a word about it. "They're good, I guess." She turned to Charlie. "Hello." She looked him over, almost as if she somehow knew who he was. But he knew there was no way she did. "Would you like something to drink?"

"I'll have a coffee," Charlie said, only because he couldn't think of anything else he wanted, and still felt a bit tired. "Maybe bring a glass of water, too, please." He smiled, keeping himself from looking at her stomach, even though he was curious.

Cody ordered an iced tea.

"I'll get those, then come back and take your order."

She walked away, and Cody leaned in over the table. He kept his voice hushed. "I'm going to go ahead and say she's pregnant."

Charlie looked over at Yona, walking around the counter. "Let's just hope Travis Crane's not the father."

Yona walked back to their table a minute later, placed the drinks down, and pulled out her pad. "Are you all set to order?"

Charlie pointed to the menu. "I'll have the turkey club with fries."

Cody nodded, handing Yona the menu. "I'll have the same."

She wrote on the pad. "Anything else?"

"I actually have a question for you," he said. "Any chance you're still involved with Travis Crane?"

Yona's big smile dropped from her face. Charlie could tell she was trying to fight off a swallow but couldn't help it. It took her a moment, but she finally shook her head. "I haven't talked to him."

"You haven't talked to him?" Charlie said. "But does that mean you're not involved with him at all? The reason I'm asking"—Charlie held his badge up, just enough so she could see it—"I'm a U.S. Marshal, and I need to know where he is. You're not in any kind of trouble, as long as you can tell us what you know about where he could be."

She pointed with her thumb over her shoulder toward the counter. "I'd love to help you if I could, but I don't know where he is. And, I'm really busy right now. I'm sorry." She turned and walked around the counter and through the swinging door to the kitchen.

"She's lying," Cody said. "You see the look on her face when you said his name?"

Charlie watched the door to the kitchen, wondering if Yona was going to come back out from it. "You think so? She looks like a scared little girl to me, but I'd have to say I agree." He looked out the window at the back of the diner and saw Yona walking across the parking lot. "Where's she going?" he said, standing from the table.

Cody turned and looked out the same window.

Charlie excused himself as he stood next to a table with four people eating their meals. He looked out the window, watching Yona. "She's making a phone call," he said, turned from the window, and hurried around the counter and through the swinging door into the kitchen.

The cooks and waitresses back there looked at him, but Charlie continued to a door he saw was only partly closed. He headed outside and over to the area of the parking lot where Yona was on the phone.

He heard her talking, her voice low: "I gotta go. He's here."

Charlie grabbed the phone from her hand and put it up to his ear. "Hello? Travis?" There was nobody on the other end. "Was that him?" he said. "Were you warning him we're here looking for him?"

She just stared back at Charlie. "He didn't do any-thing," she said.

"He kidnapped a young woman, Yona." He looked at the phone but the screen was locked. "Unlock this," he said. "I want to talk to him."

She took the phone but shook her head. "Please, I..."

Cody walked out behind Charlie. "Yona, you're go-ing to have to cooperate with the deputy. You have no choice."

"He didn't do anything. I swear. He told me he—"

"I want you to call him back," Charlie said. "Or tell me where he is."

"Is he on the Qualla?" Cody said, grabbing Yona's wrist. "Yona..."

She started to cry and an older man—the restaurant's owner—stepped out through the back door. "Chief? What's going on here? Yona? What did you do now?"

Charlie held up his badge. "U.S. Marshals Service, sir. Yona's going to need someone to take over for her in there for a few minutes."

"What's this all about?" the man said, looking at the three. "Yona?"

Cody said, "A man named Travis Crane is wanted for kidnapping a young woman in Asheville."

The man said, "Yona? Do not tell me you are still involved with that man. If your father..." He turned toward Charlie. "He kidnapped someone?"

"I guess you know who he is?"

The man nodded, his eyes on Yona. "I know of him only because Wes, her father, told me if I ever see him around her to let him know."

"Have you seen him?" Cody said.

The man shook his head. "Only one time, but that was months ago, before..." The man paused, looking down at Yona's stomach. "You can tell them," he said to her. "I have to go take care of my customers."

"Do you want to tell us what he's talking about?" Charlie said, although he already had a feeling what it was.

Tears came down Yona's cheeks as she rubbed her stomach with both hands. "He is the father of my baby."

Charlie and Cody both stood quiet.

"You can't withhold information from the marshal, Yona. You have to tell him what he asks."

She looked at Charlie, shaking her head. "I don't know where he is. He told me he had nothing to do with that girl's kidnapping."

"Well, I'm sure that's what he told you," Charlie said, handing her the phone. "But I need you to dial this phone. I want to talk to him."

"He's not going to talk to you."

He held the phone out, waiting for her to take it. "Call him back, Yona. I want you to find out where he is."

"I told him you were here. He already knows. He won't even answer."

Cody said, "Yona, dial the phone. And give us his number."

"It's not his phone," she said.

Charlie looked her in the eye. "Then whose is it?"

She shrugged. "I mean, it's not his regular phone."

"I don't care," he said. "Dial it. Or you're coming with us."

Yona cleared her throat, her hands shaking as she took the phone from Charlie and tapped the screen.

"Give it to me," Charlie said, putting out his hand. She did as he said and he placed it up to his ear, listening as the phone rang three times until finally someone answered.

"Are they still there?" the voice said.

"Travis Crane? This is Deputy U.S. Marshal Charlie Harlow." Charlie listened for a response and looked at the screen when the other line went silent.

Travis had hung up, as Charlie had expected but hoped, somehow, he could get the man to talk.

"Yona, I'm going to let you get back to work. But, just so you're aware, I'm going to your house so I can speak with your parents."

"No, please, don't tell them I was—"

"Does your father know this young man is the father of your child?" Cody said, putting his hand on Yona's shoulder.

She wiped another tear, nodding. "My father said he will kill him if he ever sees him anywhere near me."

"Then why is he calling you?" Cody said.

Yona looked at Chief Walker but didn't answer.

"I'm going to ask you one last time," Charlie said. "Do you know where he is? Or where he may be going?"

She paused, waiting, then finally shook her head. "I don't know."

"Yona. This young woman needs our help. She needs *your* help."

Yona said, "He didn't tell me. He said he doesn't have her."

"So, you knew about it?" Charlie tried to stay calm but couldn't help raising his voice. "*You knew he kidnapped another woman? And you didn't tell anyone?*"

She looked down at the gravel-covered ground. "I went to see him... he had her in a shed behind the house." After a pause, she looked up at Charlie. "But he doesn't have her anymore."

The fact she was in the shed wasn't news. But the rest of it was.

Charlie said, "What do you mean 'he doesn't have her anymore'?"

She swallowed hard, sniffling, wiping her nose with the back of her hand. "Someone else took her. They were—Travis and his uncle—they were paid by someone. He said she wouldn't be hurt, and that it was a lot of money. He said... he said he needed to do it." She gently rubbed her stomach. "For our baby."

Chapter 19

CODY WAS BEHIND THE wheel, Charlie in the passenger seat making a call to Frank, looking over his left shoulder into the back seat at Yona crying.

Charlie spoke into the phone. "She claims she doesn't know where he's gone. But maybe she'll have more to say when we get her in front of the parents."

Frank said, "You call the sheriff already?"

"Not yet. You're my first call," Charlie said. "I'm also going to need you to go by and pick up Kim, if that's all right? I told her I would, but I have a feeling Travis and his brother are somewhere out this way."

"What makes you so sure?" Frank said. "They could be anywhere. But if what she's telling you is true—and it doesn't sound to me she'd have a reason to lie about it—we've got more to worry about. You know exactly what I'm talking about."

Charlie hated to have to think about the reality of what could've happened to Haley. "I know well enough how these operations work."

Cody turned the wheel and drove up the driveway of a two-story home. He stopped behind a pickup truck parked in front of a carport, with what looked like an older Cadillac up on blocks underneath it. "Wes is a mechanic," he said, turning to Charlie as he turned the key in the ignition and killed the engine. "Best in the area."

The two stepped out of the car, and Cody opened the rear passenger door, helping Yona out from the vehicle.

Before they even made it to the door, a woman who looked similar to Yona stepped out of the house. "Chief? Yona?" She looked at Charlie. "What's going on?"

Yona's mother brushed past Charlie, taking her daughter's hand and looking into her eyes. "Yona? What happened?" She looked from Cody to Yona and over to Charlie. "Who is this?"

Tears came down Yona's cheeks.

Cody said, "Kina, this is Deputy U.S. Marshal Harlow. Kina is Yona's mother."

Charlie gave her a nod and touched the bill of his U.S. Marshals cap. "Ma'am."

Cody removed his hat, fixing his hair. "Is Wes home?" He looked toward the open front door.

"He's out back. Can you please tell me what this is all about?"

"I think you should get Wes first, so we can explain everything."

She nodded and started around the side of the house, disappearing into the backyard. The buzz of a chainsaw echoed.

"Am I going to jail?" Yona said, although she'd already asked Charlie and Cody the same question at least a half dozen times on the ride over.

"You cooperate with us," Charlie said, "we'll do everything we can to make sure you aren't." He glanced at Cody, the two knowing what Yona had done not only put another young woman's life in danger, but without a doubt broke the law, too, to protect her boyfriend.

Cody said, "You can't lie to us from here forward, do you understand?"

Yona nodded without hesitation.

A man about Charlie's size came around the corner from the side of the house, a look of concern and surprise on his face as he removed leather work gloves from his hands.

His wife walked up behind him.

"Cody?" the father said. "What's going on?" He turned and looked at his wife as she walked around the side of the house and stood next to him.

"Wes, this is Deputy U.S. Marshal Charlie Harlow," Cody said. "He—along with most law enforcement from here to Asheville—are looking for Travis Crane and the young woman he allegedly kidnapped."

Wes Cooper looked at his daughter, not saying a word at first, then turning his glance to Charlie and Cody. "Yona doesn't talk to him anymore. She has nothing to do with him. He's not allowed anywhere near her."

Charlie swallowed. "Well, Mr. Cooper, your daughter went to see him recently. And she was aware he had kidnapped Haley Moore, the woman abducted from a shopping center in Asheville."

"What do you mean 'she was aware'?" He looked at Yona. "Is this true?"

The mother let out a cry, gasping, her hands covering her mouth.

"I went to see him," Yona said, starting to explain. "I knew he was staying at his uncle's house, so I drove out there. I saw her."

"You saw who?" the father said, slight anger in his voice.

"The girl Travis kidnapped."

"Oh my God," the mother cried, the father giving her a look like he wanted her to be quiet.

He held his gaze on Yona. "You knew he kidnapped someone? And you didn't tell anyone?"

Yona shook her head, the tears starting again down her face. "He told me he'd kill me and the baby if I told anyone. He said he had no choice, he had to do it. And she wasn't going to be hurt."

The father pointed his long finger at Yona, his lips tight against his clenched teeth. "I told you never to go near him again. You should have listened to me!" He looked at Charlie and Cody, his voice calmer. "What is going to happen to her? Does it not help that she has told you the truth?"

Charlie and Cody gave each other a glance. Charlie said, "If she cooperates and helps us find him, we will do what we can to see that the judge is somewhat lenient. But, Mr. Cooper, she has put this young woman's life in danger. And I'm not sure you're aware, but Travis isn't only wanted because of the kidnapping. He's also suspected in the death of a woman whose body was found on Mount Mitchell."

The mother cried out, "I knew he was trouble from the moment Yona brought him over. I could see it: the evil in his eyes."

Wes Cooper looked Charlie in the eye. "We cannot allow you to put Yona's life in danger." He stepped toward her and put his arm around her shoulder. "She is still my little girl, even though she's made mistakes."

"I understand that," Charlie said. "But we need to find a missing young woman. She has a father out trying to find her, and he's scared, just like you. But he's scared because he doesn't know if he'll ever see his daughter again." He turned to Yona. "You may be the only person who can at least get us to Travis, or we may never find her."

The father looked somewhat puzzled. "Do you know why he's done this? Is there a ransom?"

Charlie took a breath and shook his head, hesitant to go into the details. But the father deserved to know. "I hope we're wrong, but often an abduction like this... someone like Travis and his uncle could be involved as middle men."

The father just stared back at Charlie, like he was having trouble making sense of the whole thing. "Do you mean, sex trafficking?" He shifted his eyes to Yona's stomach and placed his face in his hands.

Charlie didn't give an answer because he wanted to hope it wasn't true. Although the alternative could be that she was already dead. He didn't want to believe either scenario could be true. But he'd been a U.S. Marshal for long enough to know how these things could turn out. "All we're asking Yona to do is help bring us to him. We won't let anything happen to her."

Mr. Cooper looked at Charlie. "I knew Travis was trouble, but I had no idea. And now, Yona has to carry this man's baby. She will be punished for the rest of her life for her mistakes. But I can't allow you to use her to draw this crazy person out."

Yona was crying, and her mother stepped over and wrapped her arms around her, holding her tight and pressing her lips against the top of her head.

"Yona is not a child," Cody said, looking the father in the eye. "She could be seen as an accessory after the fact."

"But he threatened to kill her!" the mother yelled, staring Charlie in the eye while still holding Yona close to her.

Charlie nodded, shifting his stance with his hands on his hips under his jacket. "We need her help. She may be this young woman's only hope." He nodded at the father. "I will not let anything happen to her. You have my word."

Yona's phone buzzed, and she pulled it out from her back pocket to look at the screen. She had her eyes on it for a second, then looked at her father, then at Charlie and Cody. "It's Travis." She turned the screen so they could see the text message:

Are you alone?

Yona said to Charlie, "What do I say?"

"You tell him you are. Keep him talking. Don't tell him you want to see him right away, he'll be too suspicious. But don't let him disappear."

Yona stepped away from her mother and tapped the phone with her thumbs, staring at the screen.

"What did you say?" Charlie said, feeling anxious that Travis would catch on. He looked around the property, the next closest house barely visible through the trees, the mountains in the distance beyond the back of the house.

"I said I was alone. He asked what I told you. I told him nothing." She looked down at the screen again. "He wants to know how you knew it was him on the phone."

Charlie said, "Shit," somewhat under his breath, wishing he was smarter about it when he'd first learned it was Travis on the phone at the restaurant. He shouldn't have called him back at the time, but it was too late for that. "Tell him you're sorry," he said. "Tell him all you told us was you love him and that he's done nothing wrong."

She seemed to be hesitant, glancing from Charlie to her father again. Yona looked scared but started to tap the screen again. She turned it to Charlie before sending it.

He read the text:

I'm sorry, I didn't tell them anything. I would never. I love you.

"That's good," Charlie said, nodding. "Now, see what he says, then ask him when you can see him again."

Yona stared at the screen, waiting.

But Travis didn't respond. Not right away.

"What if he knows I'm helping you?" Yona said.

Charlie looked out toward the road, then back at Yona. "Call him, tell him you want to see him."

"I'm sorry, I really don't want him going near her," her father said. "The young man is crazy. I can't—"

"I promise you, I won't let anything happen."

Wes looked at Cody, looking for some kind of assurance.

"You can trust his word."

Wes said to Charlie, "If she's going to go meet him, I want to be there too."

"What?" Charlie said. "I... I can't let you do that. I mean, he sees you there, and—"

"You'll be there, won't you?" Wes said. "So then, why can't I be in the vehicle with you?"

Charlie said, "Yona, see if he'll meet you somewhere in the open. A park, or..."

"He won't come within the Qualla," she said.

"Where have you met him before?" Cody said. "There must be a place you've gone to see him?"

Yona looked at her father, hung her head, and nodded. "We've gone to a motel, out in Maggie Valley. We used to go there."

Charlie and the father exchanged a glance, and all Charlie could think was how glad he was he never had a daughter to worry about. He knew he'd never survive. "Which one?" he said, turning back to Yona.

"It's called the Smoky Falls Lodge. But what if he knows what I'm doing?" she said. "He's smart, you know. He'll know if I'm lying."

Charlie thought for a moment. "You're going to have to do all you can to make sure he doesn't know. Just act like everything's normal. I know it's easy for me to say that, but..." He glanced at the father. "Don't worry, I won't take my eyes off of her."

Yona lifted her phone and tapped the screen, then placed it next to her ear.

Charlie, Cody, and Yona's parents watched, waiting.

Yona paused, nodding. "Yes, I'm alone," she said, the first words out of her mouth. "I love you too." She listened, looking up at Charlie. "Of course I want to see you. I can leave right now." She shook her head. "No, I left work early. I couldn't wait to see you."

Chapter 20

Charlie was behind the wheel in the Suburban, Cody next to him in the passenger seat. They had dropped Yona off at the diner to pick up her blue Toyota, then stopped at the police station to swap vehicles. Driving Cody's marked car wasn't an option.

Charlie got Frank on the phone once they were on US 19, heading north and no more than a few cars behind Yona.

They'd just passed the casino when Frank answered: "Where have you been? I called you three times."

"I know. I'm sorry. We're on our way up to Maggie Valley."

"Maggie Valley? Are you going to tell me what the hell's going on? Or are you just gonna keep me and everyone else in the dark? Jesus, Charlie. You know how much I hate when you go into this Lone Ranger shit, don't you?"

"If you're done talking to me like a ten-year-old, I'll tell you where we're at." Frank was quiet on the other end, and Charlie said, "Yona Cooper had Travis Crane on the phone. And we're on our way to meet him at the Smoky Falls Lodge in Maggie Valley."

"You're on your way to *meet* Travis Crane? Are you—"

"Well, Yona's going to meet him."

Frank gave a brief pause. "Please tell me you're not using this young lady like a worm on a hook."

"He called her when we were at her parents' house," Charlie said, glancing at Cody watching him. "She told him she wants to meet him. So now we have a shot here, and I'm not going to miss it, unless you have a better idea?"

Frank said, "Have you even spoken with Sheriff Cobb about any of this? Or did you cut him out of the loop like the rest of us?"

"I didn't cut anybody out of the loop. I'm moving as fast as I have to, to get this guy into custody. You want me to drive back, fill out some forms, go talk to the sheriff, let him pull together a meeting with his deputies, then we all come back and hope Travis waits for us?"

"That's not what I'm telling you to do, Charlie. But..." He paused. "Listen, you can't just put her life in danger like this. What did you say her name was?"

"Yona. Yona Cooper."

"Okay, well you know how bad this is all going to be if something happens to Yona Cooper? Someone'll have blood on his hands, Charlie."

The line was quiet.

"Charlie? Do you hear what I'm telling you?"

Charlie yanked the wheel to the left to pass a pickup truck going under the limit, wanting to catch up with Yona going a little faster than she had been. He pushed his foot down on the gas to catch up to her. "She'll be meeting him out in the open. I told her to park in the middle of the parking lot, away from any doors or structures he can hide behind. You know I'm not going to let anything happen to her."

"What if he decides to take her somewhere else, or sniffs this whole thing out? Then what?"

"Will there ever come a time you'll stop doubting me, Frank?" Charlie looked down at his Glock in the center console. "I have Cody—Chief Walker—right here with me. I'm not alone." He looked ahead on the road and knew they were getting closer, thinking he should call Yona. "Listen, how about I call you back when we get there. Will that make you feel better, check in before we make our move?"

"I just want this son of a bitch to tell us what he's done with Haley Moore. And what about the uncle? What about him?"

Charlie shook his head. "A two for one would be nice, but I have a feeling Travis is coming alone, expecting maybe he'll get lucky with his girl." He looked at the clock on the stereo. "We're about ten minutes away from the motel. Let me run."

The line went quiet again.

"I'll call Sheriff Cobb," Frank said. "I can't imagine he's going to be happy."

"We nail Crane, we're going to be a hell of a lot closer to finding Haley than we were when Sheriff Cobb rolled out of bed this morning."

"I just need you to keep in mind, anything goes wrong, you have to remember this is Sheriff Cobb's case. Something goes wrong, it'll come down on him."

"I'm not worried about the sheriff's career," Charlie said. "But if we come out on the right side, he won't have to worry for another second about his next term."

Frank didn't respond.

Charlie was about to hang up. "Oh, Frank. What about Kim? You talk to her, let her know where things stand?"

"You say that like I actually *know* where things stand with you, Charlie." He sighed into the phone.

Charlie said, "I'm just making sure she's all right. All goes well, I can get back over there and pick her up like I promised I would."

———

Charlie stepped out of the driver's side of the Suburban, and Cody climbed over, got behind the wheel, and parked on the opposite side on Soco Street from the motel's parking lot. Charlie timed the handful of cars going each way, at a pretty good speed, and crossed to the other side. He glanced over at Yona, parked in her Toyota in the middle of the gravel parking lot, not far from the motel's entrance.

There were only a handful of vehicles parked outside, nobody inside any of them as far Charlie could tell.

He ducked down at the corner of the building and watched the road, waiting. He wasn't sure what kind of vehicle Travis would be driving. Both his uncle's Buick, with the smashed front end, and the Nissan pickup truck were in the sheriff's custody as part of the investigation.

Charlie had his Glock out by his side, poking his head out just enough to see Yona sitting in the driver's seat, looking at herself in the mirror. He was a little concerned, wondering about the girl's judgment in the first place, hoping he could trust her to do the right thing. But he knew it was too late, knowing his main goal was to keep her safe without letting Travis Crane get away. Charlie looked at his watch, with a little under ten minutes until the time Travis told Yona he'd be there.

Cody came over the two-way radio almost in a whisper. "You see that green Chevy Blazer parked on the side of the road just before the gas station?"

Charlie didn't want to stick his head out from the building so much that he'd be seen, but tried to get a look around the corner toward the road. He could see the vehicle Cody had spotted, the green SUV with Florida plates. He could make out a figure behind the wheel but couldn't get a good enough look at the face, the way the sun reflected off the tinted windows. He kept his voice low and said into the two-way, he said, "You get a look at the driver?"

"Negative," Cody said. "But he hit the brakes pretty hard, yanked the wheel at the last second to pull off the road heading south."

Charlie heard a horn blow from around the other side of the building and ran all the way around the back so he could get a better look at the parked car from the other side. He stopped short just as he got to the corner, seeing Yona step out from her car. Under his breath, he said,

"Yona, what the hell are you doing?" He had told her not to leave her car.

But that's exactly what she did, and started walking toward the parked Blazer out in the road. He watched her, the phone up to her ear as she continued across the parking lot. Charlie clicked the button on the two-way. "Cody, you see her?"

"I do, but... what is she doing?"

"I'm assuming he's got her on the phone, telling her what to do. I don't know if that means he saw us or he's just being careful, but—"

"I hope she didn't tell him we're here," Cody said. "I'd like to think Yona is smarter than that."

Charlie wasn't sure if he should jump out and make a run toward the car, or sit tight and see what Yona was going to do next. "She gets in that car, don't let him get away. You hear me?"

"I'm pulling out right now," Cody said. "I can try to block him in if—"

"No, don't. Not yet. Let's see what he's going to do." Charlie peeked across the road and saw Cody drive the Suburban out into the street, then looked back toward the parked vehicle as Yona walked up to the passenger door and opened it. He yelled into the two-way, "She's getting in!" He was about to start running across the parking lot but decided he couldn't draw attention his way. He waited, watching the Chevy Blazer. "Cody, pull back," he said. "Don't let him see you."

"You want me to wait?" Cody said, his voice coming over the two-way.

"Yes. Just hold up, or drive right past them." Charlie watched Cody go south on Soco Street past the car and into the Citgo gas station. He waited, watching, although he still hadn't been able to get a good look inside the vehicle. He wondered what the chances were the uncle was in there with the two.

The car pulled away from the edge of the road and started driving south but did a complete U-Turn, tires squealing, and headed north in the other direction at a pretty good speed.

Charlie took off across the parking lot, holstering his Glock as he ran full speed toward the Citgo station. Cody had already opened the passenger door and had the engine running. He started driving toward the road as Charlie grabbed the handle over the door from outside, running alongside the Suburban, swinging his feet up and inside and sliding into the passenger seat.

They took off after the Blazer, and Charlie looked ahead toward the road, taking his Glock from the holster and placing it on the dashboard. "Don't lose him," he said.

Cody stared ahead, doing about seventy miles an hour. "Good idea, Deputy." He reached for the two-way on his vest. "You want me to call in some help?"

Charlie wasn't sure, watching the Blazer up ahead as he thought about it. "If he doesn't know we're behind him, calling in reinforcements could backfire."

"But what if he already knows? Where are they going?"

Charlie's phone rang, and he pulled it from his pocket, looking at the screen before tossing it in the center console. "That's Sheriff Cobb," he said, ignoring the call. "I'm not about to try and explain what the hell just happened."

"They're speeding up," Cody said. "What do you want me to do?"

Charlie grabbed the Glock from the top of the dashboard and held it in his hand. "I'd say pull up next to him, I'll put a bullet in his head. But I need him alive."

"And we don't need to hurt Yona in the process of catching this man," Cody said.

Cody accelerated as the Blazer picked up speed, going at least twenty miles an hour over the limit. "We could at least call Waynesville PD, no? We might want to set up a roadblock."

Charlie said, "No. Not yet. Whatever you do, don't let them get too far ahead. We can't lose them."

They were coming up on the Clarion Hotel and Conference Center, followed by the turn for Route 276.

"Stay back a little," Charlie said.

Cody eased up on the gas and jumped on 276 North. "He's doing the speed limit now," he said.

"Just don't get too close."

Cody gave Charlie a look, like he didn't like the way he was bossing him around. "This is not my first rodeo, Deputy."

They followed for another five miles until the Blazer slowed down and turned off past the wooden sign for Windham Campground. Cody was about to pull down the same road after them when Charlie yelled, "Wait!" He pointed straight ahead. "Keep driving."

"Are you serious?" Cody said, straightening the wheel and staying north on 276. He looked at Charlie in the passenger seat. "What are you doing? Why wouldn't we—"

"I know this campground. My father took me here all the time when I was a kid. There's a back road, at least there used to be, leads into the camping spots. Back then the old man was drunk all the time, made me drive. I wasn't even thirteen." He pointed at an area that didn't look to be anything but trees, although there was a slight opening. "Turn here."

"Is it even a road?" Cody turned anyway, took the Suburban down a dirt road without a sign or any indication it would bring them anywhere but deep into the woods. The road, if it could even be called that, was completely overgrown with grass and small trees.

"Just because you were here as a kid... Can you tell me what sense it makes coming in the opposite direction? I know these woods, too, Charlie, and I'm not following your logic."

Charlie was quiet, looking straight ahead, ready to go. But he knew they needed to get closer.

They drove deeper for another two hundred or so yards.

"Stop here," Charlie said, jumping out without another word before Cody had even come to a complete stop.

He was surrounded by nothing but woods and trees. The faint sound of cars out on 276 could still be heard, but barely. He turned to close the door as Cody stopped and looked out at him. Charlie said, "Go wait by the main entrance. Don't let them out." He slammed the door closed and took off without another word.

He ran through the woods, moving fast, jumping over downed trees and bushes for at least another hundred yards under the dark canopy of leaves. He slowed up as he got closer to an area lit by streaks of sunlight with less trees overhead. He scanned the area of camp-sites—mostly empty, being close to the end of the sea-son—remembering the place from so long ago, yet still feeling like it was just yesterday he'd been there.

He stayed in the woods and walked for another hun-dred yards along the backside of the northernmost campsites. He removed his Glock from his holster when he thought he saw the green Chevy Blazer through the thickness of the trees.

Charlie kept himself low as he made his way closer, crouching down once he was close enough to get a better look. He could see someone seated on top of a picnic table.

It was Yona, but she was alone.

He tried to get closer, but it was quiet all around him. He didn't want to move until he had Travis Crane in his sights. But as much as he needed to get Crane into custody, Yona's safety had become his main concern. He knew if anything were to happen to her, it would be nobody's fault but his own.

As Frank had said, *Someone will have blood on his hands.*

And there was no question who he meant.

He tried to see into the green Blazer, but from what he could tell, even with the tinted glass, there was nobody inside. At least not in the driver's seat.

Where the hell is he?

Charlie started to doubt Crane knew Yona was trying to set him up, although, on the other hand, he started to question if Yona could potentially turn on Charlie to help her boyfriend. It was certainly a concern. Not only was she pregnant with his baby, but she clearly had a loyalty to him, going back to keeping her mouth shut, knowing he had kidnapped another young woman close to Yona's own age.

He smelled cigarette smoke and ducked down low, seeing someone walking toward Yona, he guessed had to have been Travis, coming from around the backside of the Blazer with a cigarette in his hand, blowing a stream of smoke into the air.

Travis sat down next to her, and as Charlie took another step, a twig snapped under the weight of his foot. Travis stood up and looked into the woods. "You hear that?" he said, speaking to Yona.

She turned and looked over her shoulder, almost as if staring right at Charlie. But he had ducked behind a tree, out of sight. He still wasn't far enough away for them to see him.

Charlie didn't move a muscle.

He looked at his phone to make sure the ringer was off, then turned off the two-way clipped to his jacket.

Poking his head around the tree, he could see Travis had turned away and sat down next to Yona once again.

They started to kiss: Travis with the cigarette still in his hand, the smoke rising up behind Yona where he had it resting on the table.

Charlie decided to come in at another angle and made his way another thirty yards to his left, careful with each step, until the Blazer was between him and Travis and Yona.

He started toward them, almost in a crawl over the leaves and needles, moving so slow he knew he was losing time the longer it took him to get close enough. He could still see them on the picnic table together and started to move fast enough without making a sound.

He was twenty feet from the campsite and the Blazer parked at the edge of it. He straightened up and took long steps, carefully, raising the Glock as he slowly approached the vehicle. He listened, and could hear Yona telling Travis, "No. Please, I don't want to."

"Come on, babe," Travis said. "I thought you said you missed me?" He had a passive-aggressive tone to his voice.

Charlie wanted to shoot the son of a bitch right then.

"Travis, no! Please, I don't..."

He kissed her.

Charlie poked his head out and could see Travis trying to remove her shirt. He knew he'd seen more than enough. But he was close enough now he could see the gun on the picnic table, inches from Travis.

He stepped out from behind the Blazer, the Glock raised, pointed at Travis with his sight aimed at his head. Any lower, if he had to shoot, there was too much risk of Yona being in the way. "Travis Crane, you move a muscle, I'm going to sink a piece of lead right inside that crazy-ass skull of yours." He had the gun up, in both hands. He was still. "Yona, get away from him."

But Travis wasn't letting her go. He had her arm, shaking his head without turning to look at Charlie. He flicked his cigarette away and slowly started to move his hand toward the gun.

"Don't you dare reach for your weapon," he said. "Or I'll be forced to fire mine. Believe me, I'd like nothing more than to pull this trigger."

Travis hadn't even turned to look at Charlie—his back to him—with Yona not moving, frozen, her arm in Travis's grasp.

"Please don't shoot him," Yona cried, looking at Charlie, shaking her head. "Please."

"Let her go," Charlie said, taking another step closer. He was running out of choices. He watched Travis's free hand moving closer to the gun on the table, pulling

Yona closer to him at the same time, their faces squeezed together.

Yona said, "Just do what he says. Please. He's going to shoot you."

Travis just shook his head, slowly peeking at Charlie over his shoulder as his hand jumped for the gun. He lifted it and turned the gun.

But before he came around with it, Charlie pulled the trigger. He had no option but to go for the kill, the bullet exploding from his Glock like it was all in slow motion.

Travis's head kicked back, only slightly. He fired off a shot in the air but aimed at nothing, fired another into the woods with no control at all, his body collapsing and falling to the ground from the picnic table.

Yona was screaming, crying, staring down at the body, shaking her head with her hands over her mouth.

Charlie ran to Yona and grabbed her, pulling her from the picnic table and around to the other side of the Blazer. He stepped back around and over to where Travis lay on the ground, crouched down, and felt for a pulse, knowing what he'd done was the worst possible scenario after Yona being harmed.

Travis Crane was dead.

Chapter 21

Frank had just finished yelling at Charlie when he shifted his glance through the blinds on the window behind Charlie.

Charlie turned from the chair, following Frank's eyes, and looked out into the office as Kim walked in, on crutches, and headed straight for her desk like it was just another day at work.

"What's she doing here?" Charlie said, acting like he'd already let Frank's anger roll off his chest.

Frank didn't answer, stood up shaking his head, and walked around from behind his desk. "I told her to call in from home, but I'd guess she's afraid you'll shoot someone else if she's not here to babysit you." He opened his office door and headed straight for Kim's cubicle.

Charlie followed him out, done trying to defend himself as he'd done for the past twenty minutes. It wasn't like he was unaware of the trouble that shooting Travis

Crane had caused. It *was* a real problem, and it went beyond Frank coming down on him.

Even Yona's father pointed a finger and seemed to want a piece of Charlie, with Cody Walker getting in the middle of them, having to restrain the man when he learned his only daughter was inches from the bullet Charlie had fired.

Charlie couldn't blame the man, of course. It wasn't like he wanted to kill the person who could lead him to Haley Moore.

Before they had walked from the office, Frank had said to him, "We can't afford to lose you, Charlie. But the director's wondering how we can keep someone like you around."

Charlie had heard it all before. But Frank made it clear the Justice Department had been feeling pressure to come down on the Marshals Service because of deputies like Charlie, who had somewhat of a track record for being a little too quick with the trigger.

And Sheriff Cobb didn't like the way Charlie kept him in the dark, being the last to learn Travis Crane had been shot and killed the way he had.

Frank had walked up to Kim's cubicle and leaned up against the side of it. "What are you doing?" he said, glancing over his shoulder at Charlie walking up behind him.

Charlie gave her a nod, trying to get a look at her, but Frank was blocking his view. "You feeling all right?" he said.

Frank stepped aside, and Charlie slipped inside the cubicle, leaning back against the far end of Kim's desk.

Kim looked from Frank to Charlie. "I hear Sheriff Cobb's pretty upset?"

Frank nodded. "What happened at that campground has already raised all kinds of trouble for his office. They're feeling the heat, although it's no secret Charlie was the one involved. Just a lot of questions the sheriff's having to deal with, considering they're the ones supposed to be in control of the investigation." Frank gave Charlie a nod. "Deputy Riggins is going to be keeping you on a leash," he said, looking down at her plastic-cast boot. "That's assuming she's up for it?"

Kim glanced at the crutches leaned up against the wall. "I'm fine," she said. "So is this meeting so Sheriff Cobb can come in and rip Charlie a new one? Or are we going to actually accomplish something this morning?"

Frank let out a sigh, shaking his head. "I hope he's calmed down. I mean, you can't blame the man, can you? It's all over the news, all over social media. Haley Moore's father's got his attorney involved again, going after the sheriff's office because the man who abducted her is dead, and the chances of finding her have been greatly reduced."

"That's a matter of opinion," Charlie said. "And if it weren't for me getting out there talking to Haley's old boyfriend, going out to the Qualla, we'd still be at square one. I didn't want to shoot the son of a bitch. I promise you that much."

Kim said, "Travis Crane pulled his gun. The girl... What's her name again?"

"Yona," Charlie said.

"Yona. She gave a statement that sounds to me like Charlie did what he had to. So I don't think it does anyone any good, we go around with our heads between our legs. The news is going to do the news, and social media's always going to be the cesspool it is."

Charlie gave a half smile at Kim. "I appreciate at least someone in this office will try to defend me."

Frank crossed his arms , giving Charlie a look like a disappointed parent. "You don't think I defend you? What the hell do you think I've been doing on the phone for the last hour?" He pointed his finger at Charlie. "You know what your problem is? You—"

"I *know* what my problems are, Frank. I'm well aware of all of them. I just don't think we need to get into them right now, do we?" Charlie walked out from Kim's cubicle and brushed past Frank, heading across the office to the conference room. He stopped at the doorway before he walked in. "What time's the sheriff coming in?"

Frank was already on his way back to his office. "Eight thirty."

Charlie looked at his watch and walked into the conference room, looked up at the board and the photos. He stared at each one: Jessie Redhouse, Dustin, Travis Crane, Yona, Haley... He stared at Steve Crane's photo, thinking back to the first moment he met him at the shopping center. The man seemed nice enough, telling Charlie he looked out for Haley.

He looked out for her, all right.

He stared at Haley's photo, shaking his head, then stepped over to the map up on the wall of the areas including Western North Carolina, from Charlotte to Murphy in the southwestern corner, down into Georgia and up through Tennessee and southern parts of Kentucky.

He turned and looked at Kim, standing in the doorway, then glanced at her foot. "No crutches?"

She shook her head and walked in, a bit of a wobble to her like she was trying to figure out the right way to walk in the boot. "So, what are you thinking?"

"What am I thinking?" He turned back to the map, running his finger along Route 75, running from Knoxville up to Lexington, Kentucky. "Yona said

Travis's uncle, Steve, has a friend somewhere south of Lexington. She believes that's where Travis was heading, before he came to meet her."

"No name yet?"

Charlie glanced back at her, shaking his head. "No. Not yet. Not even a town yet. It's not Lexington, but south of it. Could be any of those small towns.

"If I hadn't had to spend the whole night and into the morning dealing with everyone whining about Crane being shot, I'm sure I could've found something by now." He looked at his watch again. "I'll be honest. I'm not looking forward to the sheriff and his deputies coming in here. I hope it's not hostile, or I'll walk right out."

"Don't you think it's just to get everyone involved on the same page?"

"I hope so," Charlie said. "I know they're supposed to be in charge, but it's like having a sack of concrete on your back."

"I'm not sure that's fair," Kim said. "They're good men. Just because they follow the law doesn't make them—"

"It's not about following the law," Charlie said. "That's not what I mean. I understand that procedures and rules need to be followed. But I'm just starting to think this is beyond their scope. Don't you?"

Kim stepped closer and stood next to Charlie, elbow to elbow, looking at the map. "Frank isn't going to let you do it alone, if that's what you're thinking. Even if I'm with you, Frank doesn't want you to have free rein, for more reasons than one."

"That's not what I'm saying," he said. "But..." His phone rang and he looked at the screen, saw it was Cody. "Sorry," he said, tapping the screen to answer. "Hey, Cody."

"I spoke to Yona's father this morning," he said.

"Is he still mad?"

"Less so at me. I'm not sure he's a big fan of the U.S. Marshals Service right now, however. He will likely shoot you, you try to talk to his daughter again."

"Well, then hopefully you won't mind being the go-between," Charlie said. "Because, as hysterical as she was all night, I'd like to think she still has some talking to do. They were in that car together for a good twenty minutes."

"Well, that's why I'm calling," Cody said. "Yona mentioned the Redhouse brothers, and she believes they might know who the man is that Travis's uncle might've gone to see, up there in Kentucky."

"No shit?" Charlie said. He looked up at the photos on the board in front of him, going from the one of Jessie

Redhouse to the one of his brother, Dustin. "Did she say anything else?"

"Well," Cody said. "She's scared. She wants to know if she's going to jail."

"Yona?" Charlie shook his head, the phone to his ear. "I'd like to think we can help avoid that. I'm going to do all I can. Frank's going to see what he can do, but I just hope she knows she—"

"She knows, Charlie. She regrets every aspect of it. She's just a kid."

Charlie nodded. "I know." He thought for a moment, wishing he could go back, do it all over again. He looked at Haley's photo. "I appreciate the call, Cody. You hear anything else, call me right away. I gotta sit through some bullshit meeting this morning so Sheriff Cobb'll feel like he's in charge."

"I thought he was in charge," Cody said.

"Well, yeah, he is. But this is, I don't know... seems to me right now he's more interested in something to feed the media, make sure he doesn't slip in the polls." He looked at Kim looking back at him with an expression like he needed to keep his mouth shut.

Cody said, "I'll be standing by, whatever you need."

The two hung up, and Charlie said to Kim, "Redhouse brothers may know the man up there near Lexington, where Crane may've been going."

"Cody said that?" she said.

"Apparently Yona told her father, and he called Cody this morning." He tapped Jessie Redhouse's photo. "I'm still not convinced they've had nothing to do with any of this. But at this point, we're running out of time. I just hope either one will cooperate, tell us if they know anything else."

"Without you breaking any noses or shooting someone," Kim said, a slight smirk on her face.

Charlie turned to the conference room table. "You think it'd be bad if we're not here when the sheriff shows up?"

"Are you serious?" Kim said, almost with a laugh, but not a speck of humor to it. "This is still his case, Charlie. There's no way you can show that kind of disrespect by not being here."

"Well, the longer we sit around, the greater the chance is we're never going to find Haley Moore. You know how it is, don't you? The way most people just want to have meetings and talk about this and that all day when, the truth is, they're afraid of doing anything else that might turn out to be the wrong move."

"You mean, your exact opposite?" Kim said. "I'd say there's a middle of the road, wouldn't you agree?"

Charlie looked at the screen of his phone. "I was tempted to call Stan, see if we're coming to a point the bureau could see us moving this federal. I mean, we went from city police to the county sheriff's office. But"—he turned to the map—"if Frank's not going to try and pull it into our office, on account of ruffling Sheriff Cobb's feathers, then maybe it's time the FBI's involved."

"I don't think that's your call," Kim said.

"No, but I can at least get Stan's thoughts on it. No?"

Kim shook her head but didn't exactly give a clear answer. "You know how it is, every time you make a shift like that from one organization to another, it'll do nothing but set us back."

"I'm not saying it should necessarily be taken out of anyone's hands at this point, but if it gets pushed to the federal level, we can bring more manpower on from within USMS. Frank doesn't want me to act like the Lone Ranger, but he won't give me anyone else." He grinned. "No offense, Deputy, but you have to admit you're a bit hobbled."

Kim stared back at Charlie, shaking her head. "I'm not going to be much use if we have to chase someone on foot, but please don't insult me by—"

"You know I wouldn't want anyone else by my side," he said. "Don't take it the way it came out."

Kim looked out the doorway into the rest of the office. With her voice low, she said, "I'm all for getting out of here, go talk to the Redhouse brothers and maybe head up into Kentucky. But we can't disappear before the sheriff gets here. You know how bad that would look? Frank would have both our asses in a sling."

Charlie was surprised, his eyebrows up high. "I thought you were supposed to be the one holding the leash around my neck?"

She nodded, looking up at the map. "We have to find Haley, Charlie. If there's ever been a time I'd be willing to give you the slack you need to cross a line, it's now."

Chapter 22

With the sun coming down into his eyes over the trees, Charlie turned into the driveway, behind Jessie and Dustin's aunt's mobile home. There were no vehicles parked out front.

After the meeting with Sheriff Cobb and two of his deputies was cut short, they all followed Charlie out to Weaverville to get what they'd all hoped would be a critical piece of information from Jessie and Dustin.

But they knew the Redhouse brothers wouldn't be easy to crack, and Charlie assured Sheriff Cobb he'd let him take charge, do what he felt was right to get either brother to talk.

Kim and Charlie both stepped out from the Suburban and waited for Sheriff Cobb and Frank, driving up behind them in the sheriff's vehicle.

Deputy Carson pulled up next and parked out in the street.

Charlie leaned and whispered to Frank, "You sure I can't just go ahead and kick in the door?"

Frank gave Charlie a look like he was going to smack him, shaking his head.

Charlie stepped out of the way and let Sheriff Cobb go up to the front door ahead of them, to make it clear he understood the sheriff was in charge.

That was partially what Frank had tried to tell Charlie, that playing politics was part of the game, and it could make everyone's life a little easier if he'd give it a try.

The sheriff knocked on the frame of the aluminum screen door, turning his ear to it, as if trying to listen for something on the other side. "Those two boys'd better be here," he said. "That was part of the agreement." He knocked again, a little harder this time.

Charlie and Frank exchanged a look but turned to the door when it finally opened.

Jessie was standing on the other side, looking out through the torn screen, wearing nothing but a pair of white underwear, hair shooting out in all directions. He looked stunned and half asleep, looking out at everyone, squeezing his eyes like he was trying to clear the fog.

The sheriff said, "Jessie, we need to have a word with you and your brother."

"Dustin's in bed," he said, letting out a yawn and stretching his skinny, long arms as he rubbed his chest. "So was I."

"Well, that's too bad," Sheriff Cobb said. "Because we need to talk."

"What about? We ain't done nothin'."

Sheriff Cobb kept his calm demeanor. That's just how he was, but Charlie knew the man had to have a boiling point, like anyone else might. Maybe not a point as low as Charlie's, but...

"I'm only going to ask you one more time," the sheriff said. "Go get your brother and get yourself dressed. We're coming inside."

Jessie stared out at the sheriff, shaking his head. "You got a warrant?"

The sheriff stood almost sideways in front of the door, enough where Charlie could see the look on his face and the way the color changed to a darker shade of red.

Without another word, the sheriff's hand shot through the broken screen and grabbed Jessie by the throat, almost yanking him out. But Jessie was stuck halfway through as the door ripped off its hinges.

The sheriff tossed Jessie and the door to the ground, then leaned over and grabbed Jessie, flipped him so his face was down in the dirt, and slapped the handcuffs on his wrists.

"What the hell did I do?" Jessie cried. "Jesus Christ, you're hurtin' me."

Sheriff Cobb looked past Charlie, Frank, and Kim, and at Deputy Carson. "Deputy, go get Dustin out of bed, will you please?"

Mike Carson went inside the home, and the sheriff picked Jessie up off the ground and tossed him into a folding lawn chair by the unlit firepit with beer cans scattered all around it.

As Jessie hit the chair, he tipped over, unable to catch his fall with his hands cuffed behind his back.

The sheriff reached for him and lifted him to a seated position with the chair. He turned to Charlie. "I'd say Jessie's ready to talk now."

Charlie enjoyed the scene and was more than pleased to see the sheriff didn't have it all together the way he portrayed. It was a side of Sheriff Cobb he'd never seen.

Deputy Carson came out through the front door with Dustin ahead of him but not putting up much of a fight. He looked to be mostly asleep, like he didn't have a clue exactly what was going on.

The sheriff grabbed Dustin by the arm and tossed him into the other folding lawn chair next to his brother.

Dustin looked at his brother. "Jessie? What'd you do?"

Jessie said, "I didn't do nothin'," looking around at everyone watching him.

"Deputy," the sheriff said, giving Charlie a nod. "You want to see what you can get?"

Charlie stepped forward, getting up close to Jessie's face, examining the swollen nose. He leaned forward with his hands down on his knees, close enough he could smell Jessie's body odor. "How's the nose?"

"It's broken, you son of a bitch." Jessie had a snarl on his face and stared Charlie in the eye.

"Looks like it's healing up all right," Charlie said. "But I'd hate to see what it'd look like if it happened again." He straightened up, his hands on his hips. "You know what I'm trying to say?"

"What the hell do you want?" Jessie said.

"What we'd like you to tell us is the name of the man you know up in Kentucky, lives somewhere south of Lexington, who also happens to know Travis Crane and his uncle."

Jessie and Dustin both exchanged a look. "Why?"

Charlie let out a sigh, trying to keep himself calm without re-breaking Jessie's nose. "I'm going to ask you one more time." He glanced at Dustin. "Feel free to speak up anytime, Dustin. But I want one of you to answer. If I have to ask a second time..." He stared into Jessie's eyes. "What is the name of the man you know, lives up south of Lexington, Kentucky. He knows Travis's uncle, Steve Crane."

Jessie and Dustin sat in silence for a moment until Jessie finally snorted, cleared his throat, and spit on the ground, missing Charlie's boot by no more than a handful of inches. "Darnell Roberts."

"Darnell Roberts?" Charlie looked over at Frank, then Kim. "You got that?"

Kim had her phone out, dialing.

The sheriff stepped toward Jessie. "You have an address?"

Jessie shook his head. "I'm not sure the street or nothing, but I can tell you where the house is. It's a farm."

"What about the girl?" the sheriff said, grabbing Jessie by one of his arms, twisting him around with the way his hands were behind his back. "Is that where they brought her? Haley Moore?"

Jessie started to shake his head, but Dustin spoke up. "I wouldn't be surprised."

The sheriff pushed himself past Charlie and grabbed Dustin by the arm. "Why didn't you tell us this before? You little piece of shit."

"I... I didn't know. I swear. I mean, I don't know, I—"

"It's true," Jessie said. "We don't know if she's there or not." He looked from Charlie to the sheriff, both towering over the two brothers. "He mighta had something to do with some kind of operation, like always had these young, pretty girls workin' for him. Some, I don't know how true it is, but some he mighta sold or something."

Charlie said, "Are you telling me this guy's a sex trafficker?"

Kim held the phone out from her ear. "We have an address for Darnell Roberts."

Frank looked from Charlie to Sheriff Cobb. "We oughta give a heads-up to law enforcement up there. I can go ahead and reach out, give Colonel Lewis a call."

Sheriff Cobb nodded. "I spoke with him when we first broadcast the missing persons alert, same night we took it over from Asheville. He assured us as much manpower from the state police as we'd need."

Charlie put his finger up in the air, as if asking for attention. "Now, hold on one moment," he said. "I'm not certain we're at a point yet we go all in with thirty men and women, guns blazing, copters flying overhead. I don't doubt we need local law enforcement up there on alert, at the very least have the highways and roads under patrol, but we don't want to draw any unnecessary attention just yet, do we?" He looked at Frank, waiting for his thoughts.

Frank and Kim both nodded, like they agreed, but Frank already had the phone up to his ear. "I'll get 'em on standby."

Charlie looked in the rearview at the line of cars behind him on I-40 just below Knoxville. Sheriff Cobb was directly behind him followed by Frank next in the pickup truck. Another four sheriff's vehicles followed. He glanced down at the speedometer, doing close to eighty, doing what he could to cut down on the nearly four-hour drive into the small town of Tyner, Kentucky.

Kim turned in the passenger seat to look out the back of the Suburban. "Where are we meeting?"

Charlie nodded, glancing at Kim with the laptop in front of her. "Six minutes away from the house, a church in Annville, off Route Thirty-Six-Thirty. Frank said a dozen troopers will be there, from Kentucky State Police." He looked down at the cast boot on Kim's foot. "Can you drive with that thing?"

"It's my left leg," she said, nodding. "No problem at all. But don't think of me as useless out there, Charlie. I can move just fine. If I brought my other shoe, I'd think about taking this boot off altogether."

"Might just need you to wait in the vehicle," he said, giving her a small grin. "Don't take it personally."

Kim looked down at the laptop in front of her. "Looks like the farm where he lives was owned by family, and appears to be a working farm, but with no active business record of any kind. And from what it looks like from here, he's clean. No criminal record comes up." She tapped the keys on the laptop. "The connection's going in and out." After a moment, she looked at Charlie. "He's military. U.S. Army. He served in Afghanistan for six years."

Charlie gave her a quick glance as he picked up his phone and tapped the screen to call Frank.

Frank answered, "Yeah?"

"Darnell's military," Charlie said. "A marine. Served in Afghanistan."

Kim was still on the laptop. "He served with Steve Crane, trained together at Fort Campbell in Hopkinsville."

"You hear that?" Charlie said. "He may have trained with Steve Crane."

Chapter 23

THE SUN WAS WARM, beating down on the church parking lot filled with fourteen vehicles and at least twenty-five law enforcement officials: twelve Kentucky state troopers and six deputies from Buncombe County, plus three deputy U.S. Marshals in addition to Charlie, Kim, and Frank. Three deputies from Jackson County were on their way.

Charlie and Frank had the map out on the hood of Frank's pickup truck, pointing out the various roads and highways they best felt should be blocked to prevent Darnell Roberts and Steve Crane from getting anywhere other than on foot.

Charlie said, "We'll want someone up here just south of the elementary school on Nance Road; get a car over here at the corner of Nance and Red Davidson Road." He ran his finger along the map. "If we could get three or four vehicles along Conway Road, north of the farm... maybe even a fifth to make sure nobody comes out of there unseen, either man slips away from us. Maybe another two vehicles patrolling Thirty-Six-Thirty, running north and south." He turned from the map. "We box them in this area, they'll have a slim chance of getting beyond any of these roads. Anyone not in a parked vehicle would patrol." He turned again to the map. "Just keep working around this area. We'll report as soon as we have the vehicles identified."

Charlie glanced at Sheriff Cobb who had, at that point, just about taken a back seat to Charlie and Frank and appeared to be all right with it. As he told Charlie, when they both stepped out of their vehicles, "My only concern at this point is finding Haley Moore. If it means I lose an election, so be it."

After the details were handed out, and all roads leading to and from the farm off Conway road were covered, Charlie jumped into the passenger seat with Kim behind the wheel of his Suburban. Frank followed in his truck with a state trooper and Sheriff Cobb in two separate vehicles behind them.

Charlie and Kim were both quiet on the five-minute drive to the farm until Kim turned down the long driveway. The house was set back a ways but could be seen through the trees.

Charlie turned to look behind him at Frank with the sheriff. The two troopers stopped at the end of the driveway, blocking the entrance.

Kim drove up behind a full-size Ford pickup truck, and an older Audi with faded paint and a touch of rust around the lower part, parked next to it. The truck had a Kentucky registration plate, but the Audi's was North Carolina. Both were parked in front of a building separated from the house and had three closed garage doors on the front.

Before either stepped out, Charlie checked both plates on the computer. The truck was registered to Darnell Roberts, but the other—the one from North Carolina—had been registered to a Mrs. Clara Johnson but had been reported stolen. "Look at that," Charlie said, pushing open the passenger door. He turned to Kim. "Sit tight, all right? Anyone tries to take off, they won't get very far. But if you decide to give chase, I'd appreciate it if you don't leave me behind like last time."

"When did I leave you behind?" Charlie pulled his cap down tight on his head and thought about it, then smiled. "Oh, right. You were the one I left behind." He closed the door and looked back at Frank, pulling his holster over his shoulder as they walked across the dusty driveway toward the front door.

The house was two stories, modest in size but had a nice country porch with a couple of rocking chairs. Chickens walked freely around the front of it, pecking at the ground.

Charlie and Frank both looked out toward an area on the farm where there were at least twenty or so people out in the fields picking crops. "We want to try the door?" Frank said. "Or go see what's going on over there?"

But before either had a chance to decide, the front door opened, and a man stepped out, tall and in good shape from where Charlie stood, wearing a pair of overalls. He wore a T-shirt underneath, showing off his softball-sized biceps. "Can I help you?" the man said, his hands tucked in his pockets.

Charlie and Frank both pulled their badges, and Charlie said, "U.S. Marshals Service. Are you Darnell Roberts?"

The man nodded once.

Charlie said, "We'd like to ask you a few questions, if you have a few minutes?"

The man looked at the badges, then over at the Suburban with Kim in the front seat. "What about?" he said, slowly walking down the steps.

Charlie looked out toward the workers in the field. "What kind of crops you growing?" He looked beyond the field toward a barnlike structure set far back, almost into the woods.

The man rubbed the back of his neck, his muscle bulging like he was purposefully flexing to show off his size. "We grow plenty year-round. Right now, broccoli's at its peak, got cabbage out there. Beets and turnips, but rain's been scarce, really hurting the greens." He nodded toward the chickens. "Of course, they produce eggs for us year-round."

Frank said, "Darnell, is this your main business?"

There was a brief pause.

"Excuse me?"

"I'm just asking if this is all you do? Run the farm?"

Darnell took a moment before he answered. "You could say that."

"Oh," Frank said.

Charlie stepped over to the Audi and tried to open the door. "Is this your car?"

Darnell cleared his throat and didn't even try to answer. "You mind telling me what you two gentlemen would like? I'm a busy man, and—"

"Where's Steve Crane?" Charlie said, putting his hand on his hip to show his gun holstered there. He nodded toward the car. "You want to explain to us why you have a stolen vehicle on your property?"

Darnell stayed quiet, looking behind him toward the house. "It's a friend's."

"This stolen vehicle belongs to a friend?" Frank said, looking around the property. "Any chance this so-called friend happens to be here?"

Frank shook his head. "No." He gave Charlie a quick glance.

Charlie said, "So your friend showed up, left a stolen vehicle in your driveway, then disappeared?"

Darnell didn't answer.

"You want to play a game?" Charlie said. "How about I try to guess your friend's name?"

Frank said. "I'd like to play."

"You have a warrant?" Darnell said. "If not, I'd like you to leave."

"Well, see, Darnell. We show up and find a stolen vehicle on your property, we don't technically need a warrant. That's just not how it works."

"Are we still playing the game?" Frank said. "I'd like to go first, maybe take a guess... oh, I don't know... I'll go with Steve Crane... just to pull a name out of thin air."

"Good guess," Charlie said, glancing at Frank, then turned to Darnell, waiting to see his reaction. "You want to tell us where he is?"

Darnell said, "I don't know who that is."

"Oh no? I'm guessing he's the man who stole this car to drive out here. You may have also seen his name pop up on the news, man who's wanted for kidnapping?"

Charlie could see the man was thinking through his options, his eyes moving around the yard like he was trying to think of what to do.

Kim had stepped out of the Suburban and left the driver's-side door open, standing behind it watching them.

Charlie knew she had her gun out, then pulled his.

Frank said, "Why don't you turn around, Mr. Darnell, and put your hands up on your head."

But as Frank detached the handcuffs from his belt and started toward Darnell, rapid gunshots were fired from someone inside the house, hitting the dirt and the Suburban's grill.

Charlie and Frank both turned and ran for cover as more shots were fired from what was clearly an automatic weapon. The two hit the ground with a cloud of dust around them, crawling to the back of the Suburban.

Kim ducked for cover with them, and Charlie poked his head around to get a look, but Darnell had already disappeared.

Frank said to Charlie, "I was sure you were going to shoot Darnell in the back."

Charlie knew he certainly *wanted* to but needed the man alive, just as much—if not more—than he needed

Travis Crane alive. He looked up toward the house when another shot fired, this time seeing someone with a shotgun poking out from one of the second-floor windows. "We need them alive," he said.

Another round of shots were fired, and Charlie was on the two-way. "We need assistance," he said. "Right away. Suspects on the move." He looked toward the crop field and could see the people who were working out there had all disappeared. A handful could be seen running into the woods. "Jesus," he said. "You see this?"

Frank and Kim both looked toward the field, the remaining few workers scattered around the property running, many into the barn.

"They're either escaping, or—"

A motor had started from somewhere either inside the garage or around the back of it. It was the sound of a motorbike. Charlie got to his feet and looked through the rear window of the Suburban and out the front toward the structure next to the house. "Shit!" he said, running out from behind the Suburban, toward two men on motorbikes.

The bikes both kicked up dust behind them, engines whining—*bwahhhh, bwahhhhh, bwahhhh*—both bikes speeding across the farmland away from Charlie. He knew from the green trim that the bikes were Kawasakis.

He raised his Glock, wanting to fire a shot at one of them—if not both—but it wasn't worth the risk. He turned and ran back toward Frank and Kim.

Kim was already in the front seat of the Suburban, the engine running. "Let's go!"

Frank was on the two-way, hurrying for his truck. "Both suspects are on motorbikes heading east toward Conway Road."

Charlie was about to get in the passenger side of the Suburban but stopped, turned, and looked at the house. "You and Frank go ahead without me."

Kim didn't even ask, like she knew exactly what he was thinking, then spun the Suburban around, tires kicking up the dirt and a cloud of dust all around it. She took off full speed down the driveway toward the road.

Frank took off, too, maybe not even noticing Charlie had stayed behind.

Charlie looked toward the farm and saw a man coming toward him with a shotgun in his hand. But when Charlie raised his gun, the man dropped his weapon and took off in the other direction. "Stop!" Charlie yelled, running after him, not knowing who the man was.

But there was no way he was going to let this one get away.

He chased after him, the little man moving fast, but Charlie caught up to him..Close enough now, he dove, fully extended, and tackled the man from the back. Charlie brought him down, and the two rolled on the ground and into the woods, just past the crops.

"No, señor," the man said. "Por favor no me dispares."

Charlie had the man by the shirt and pulled him up from the ground, holding the gun in his face. He knew enough Spanish to know the man was asking him not to shoot him. It was a simple request, but one Charlie would sometimes ignore.

He dragged the man out from the crops toward the house, then pushed him ahead with the Glock at the man's back. Charlie tried to think through the language, hoping he could communicate enough to at least get some answers.

He made it out to the driveway with the man and threw him up against the stolen car. "What are you doing here?" Charlie said, in English, thinking through what little he knew in Spanish. He asked him what his name was: "Cómo te llamas?"

The man said, "Carlos."

"You don't speak English?" Charlie said.

The man shrugged. "Un poquito." But the man also gestured with his hand, as if to say so-so.

"Do you live here?" Charlie said, pointing to the house. "Tu casa?" asking if it was the man's house, although all he wanted to know was if he lived there. The man turned and pointed to the barn off in the distance, in front of the woods beyond the farm area with the vegetable crops.

"You live there?" Charlie said.

The man nodded.

"You work here? On the farm?"

The man nodded again. "Sí."

Charlie pulled out his phone and brought up a photo of Haley, turned it to the man, and right away could see in the man's eyes he recognized her. "Do you know her?"

The man seemed to hesitate a moment, then finally nodded, and pointed toward the house behind them.

Chapter 24

Charlie was inside the old house, at first being careful but picking up his pace. "U.S. Marshals," he said, holding his Glock up in front of him. He looked in the first room he saw, with a couch and two matching chairs and a coffee table between them. "Hello?"

There was a slight breeze coming through, with most, if not all of the windows wide open. There was a smell he wasn't sure came from outside, from the farm, or if it was something in the house. He couldn't quite place the odor, although it grew stronger once he noticed it, like something from a garbage truck driving by on a hot, humid summer day.

He walked down the hall toward the back of the house as flies flew at his head. He swatted them away, stepping into the large farmhouse kitchen with an island in the middle of it with a pile of bloodied red meat and a butcher's knife. He could only assume it was a cow being butchered in the man's kitchen, with the blood around it soaking into the newspapers beneath the meat. There were a pair of long rubber gloves on the counter and a rubber apron stained with blood hung on a hook on the wall by the doorway behind Charlie.

The odor was stronger where he stood, but the smell didn't seem to come from the meat on the island. He stepped around and on the other side of the island, next to a wooden stool, was a plastic barrel, stained and filthy on the sides. It was filled with meat and discarded scraps from the butchered animal, flies all around it. It was the source of the odor, and Charlie had to cover his face with his arm to keep it from making him sick.

He wondered what else could be inside that barrel to make it smell like that, considering the top of it appeared to be as freshly cut as the meat on the island.

Charlie opened the refrigerator door, and inside it were dozens of various-sized packages wrapped in green butcher paper, closed with a single piece of masking tape.

He closed the door and went from the kitchen to the dining room with a large chestnut table and eight chairs in the middle. A hutch against the wall was filled with what looked like mostly silver, from platters to dishes and cups. The room appeared to have been untouched and not used.

He walked through the doorway on the other side and into a room with a small television with rabbit ears on the top. It was an old, small TV of the kind Charlie hadn't seen in at least twenty years.

He moved through the other rooms on the first floor and didn't find a sign of anyone, then hurried up the stairs and stopped in the hallway at the top. Straight ahead of him was an open door to a bathroom. He went in and right away opened the shower curtain, raising his gun at the same time. He looked in at an empty shower stall, although the tub appeared wet with beads of water on the surface.

Back in the hall, he walked toward an open door at one end. Raising his Glock, he carefully stepped inside. "U.S. Marshals," he said. "Anybody here?"

The bed was unmade, and clothes were piled on a chair in the corner. There was a large dresser with at least a dozen drawers, but he didn't bother going through them.

He thought maybe he should have brought the Spanish-speaking man, Carlos, inside with him, but instead left him handcuffed to the railing outside on the porch.

Charlie looked under the bed and in the closet, but there was nobody in the bedroom.

He walked down the other end of the hall. There were two doors and both were closed. He tried the one on the right, slowly turning the knob and stepping into a dark room. The blinds were closed and the windows were down. The room smelled of sweat and body odor.

He flicked on the light and walked to the unmade bed, the sheets and blankets lumped up against the wall. He nudged it with the muzzle of his gun, just in case.

There was a closet door he walked toward, his Glock ready as he turned the knob. He pulled it open but it, too, was empty.

He stepped across the hall to the other room and pushed the door open with his foot. "Hello?"

The room was bright and empty, other than a small folding table and folding chair tucked underneath it. On top of it were wires he was sure had plugged into a computer or laptop. The one window in the small room was wide open, without a screen on the other side. On the floor, in front of it, were empty shotgun shells, Charlie knowing whoever was inside the house shot at him from that very room.

There was no sign of Haley or anyone else. The room didn't have a closet.

He was on his way down the stairs to see if he could get Carlos to talk. Charlie tried to ask him, at first, where Haley was in the house. He either didn't understand the question or didn't know.

He heard a thump from somewhere on the first floor and ran the rest of the way down the stairs. He turned toward the kitchen and heard it again, but it was coming from the floor, almost right below where he stood.

He looked for a door to a basement, but the first time he walked around the lower floor, he didn't see one. He ran outside and grabbed the man, Carlos, by the shirt. "Where is she?"

He just shrugged, shaking his head with the look of fear on his face.

"Then how do you know she's here?"

He stared at Charlie without an answer, and Charlie pushed him away, the man falling to the porch floor but not going far, his hands cuffed to the railing.

Charlie ran around to the back of the house and saw where the windows were boarded up with plywood. He continued past steps leading to a back door to the other side of the house, where at least a half cord of split wood was piled up against the exterior. It was grayed and didn't appear to be recently cut. He looked closer and saw a brown tarp underneath the wood. It looked as if something was covered. Whatever it was, it didn't look right.

He picked up a piece of wood, then another, and started tossing them away from the pile. He'd gotten enough cleared, he was able to pull at the tarp and lift most of it so that he could see what was covered.

The bulkhead leading to the basement was buried under the wood. Charlie moved as fast as he could, clearing all of it in under ten minutes, getting enough removed he could get to the steel doors. But there was a chain running through the handle and a lock holding it closed. He looked around for a way to open the bulkhead. He spotted a rusted spade leaning up against the house, just a few feet away, grabbed it by the wooden handle and wedged it under the lock. He pushed down with enough pressure, the handle snapped in his hand. He tossed the broken piece to the ground, ran around to the front of the house expecting to see his Suburban in the driveway. But he'd forgotten, for a brief moment, Kim had taken it to track down the two suspects.

Charlie tried the driver's-side door of the old Audi and reached for the lever to pop the lid on the trunk. He hurried around to it, reached into the trunk, and took out the tire iron, running back around to the bulkhead.

He stuck the tire iron into the shank of the lock and tried to twist and snap it open, but it wouldn't budge. He got his fingers underneath the bulkhead doors and tried to pull to lift it but without luck, then again whacked the lock several times with hard, fast swings.

It wouldn't open.

He pounded on the bulkhead. "Haley? Are you down there? Can anyone hear me?" He turned to listen with his good ear, but the only sound came from a sudden breeze cutting through the trees.

He took his phone from his pocket and dialed Kim.

"They're gone," she said, as soon as she answered.

He wasn't as concerned with catching the two. Not right then. "Haley's in the basement."

"You found her?"

"I think so," he said, then without a thought pulled his Glock from his holster, pointed it at the lock and fired a shot. He busted the lock open and said, "I'll call you back."

"We're on our way back now," she said.

Charlie kicked the busted lock away with his boot and reached down, lifting open the bulkhead door. He hurried down the stairs, ducking his head as he stepped into the dark, musty basement. The first room he was in was enclosed with dark paneled walls and a concrete floor. There was a single door leading from the room, and he dropped his shoulder into it, busting it from the hinges. The next room he walked into was pitch black. He used the light on his phone to look for a switch and saw a string hanging from a single bulb on the low ceiling. He yanked the string and saw yet another door he hurried toward, again driving his shoulder into it.

The next area in the basement was a much larger space with an old, yellow leather couch and round wooden table with four chairs around it. He saw a switch on the wall and turned on the overhead fluorescent light, circling the room with his eyes until he spotted what looked like a walk-in cooler, the kind restaurants had. There was another lock on it, but he didn't want to fire his Glock. Not yet.

He banged on the door to the cooler. "Haley?"

There was no answer.

He yelled her name again, pounding on the door.

A cry came from the other side. "Help!"

"Back away from the door!" he yelled. "Do you hear me? I'm going to fire my weapon to get it open." Again, he said, "Do you hear me?"

"Yes," the voice said from the other side.

Charlie pulled his Glock, fired two shots at the lock and kicked it off. He opened the door and at first saw darkness, until the light behind him glowed on two young women looking out at him with big eyes, scared to move.

A third stepped out from behind them, and Charlie felt a chill run through his body as he hurried toward her.

Haley Moore ran into his arms without a word and cried.

Chapter 25

THERE HAD TO HAVE been twenty-five police vehicles and at least three rescue trucks parked up and down the driveway and toward the field with the vegetable crops. Haley and the other two females—one older, one younger—were taken to Baptist Health Hospital in Lexington. Charlie didn't wait for Sheriff Cobb or anyone else to call Haley's father to let him know she'd been found.

Most of the workers who had scattered when the gunshots were first fired were found hiding in the barn at the back of the property, beyond the field. It turned out the only job Carlos had, for which he was paid a small amount of money and given a place to sleep, was to see to it none of the workers escaped. Although most never tried to leave.

Charlie leaned against his Suburban facing Frank and Kim and nodded toward the field where the workers were being rounded up. "Twenty-nine people living together in that barn back there, sharing old mattresses spread all around the floor and a single outhouse out back. The place smelled as bad as the barrel of rotting meat inside that house."

Frank said to Kim, "Reminds me of that trafficking network, down Georgia: victims were smuggled up from Mexico, forced to pick onions."

Kim nodded. "Similar conditions, but five times as many victims were held up in a place smaller than that barn."

Charlie said, "Paid them something like twenty cents for every bucket of onions they picked. Wasn't that right?"

Frank turned to look toward the workers being led from the barn onto a long school bus. "Not sure this was what those people had in mind when they learned they'd get a chance to come to America."

Charlie said, "The American dream is a powerful attraction when you're desperate."

"You say it like they came here by choice," Kim said. "These poor victims are exploited by people like Darnell Roberts, who'll do whatever it takes to put money in their pockets."

"All driven by greed," Charlie said. "Welcome to America."

Sheriff Cobb walked over and lifted the waist of his pants, standing in front of Charlie. "I've gotta give you credit," he said. "You're not one to ever give up."

"I prefer not to," Charlie said. "But we're not done *yet*."

Sheriff Cobb took his hat off and scratched his head. "I realize that, Deputy." He turned to look toward the house as two agents in blue jackets with "FBI" in yellow letters on the backs, walked around from the side of the house and in the front door.

Frank said, "Although this has moved well beyond Buncombe County and been escalated to the federal level, we're all still going to need all the help we can get from you and whatever deputies you may have available. The director has agreed to deputization, but we'd need to start the process as soon as possible."

"Come on, Frank." Charlie said. "We don't have time to deal with the red tape of interagency coordination," He turned to the sheriff. "We just need to get moving. We'll take whatever help we can get, worry about the details later."

Kim looked at Charlie, shaking her head. "You forget what happened last time you tried to go over the director's head?"

The sheriff's phone rang, and he pulled it from the holder on his belt. "Excuse me," he said, then answered,

"Sheriff Cobb." He listened, nodding his head. "All right, thank you, Sheriff. But I'm going to hand you off to Chief Deputy Frank Carter, with Northwestern Carolina's office of the U.S. Marshals Service. He'll be overseeing the fugitive search." He handed Frank his phone. "It's Sheriff Andy Green, Owsley County."

Frank nodded, cracking a slightly crooked smile. "Sheriff Green," he said, taking the phone. "Been a long time," he said, stepping away from the others to take the call.

Sheriff Cobb said to Charlie and Kim, "He's calling because someone reported two Kawasaki motorbikes coming out of the woods behind a cemetery, southeast of Booneville."

"Booneville?" Kim said. "What's that, about twenty miles from here?"

"That sounds about right," Charlie said, looking toward the barn to the left of the house. "That's a decent trip on a single tank of gas." He thought for a moment. "This escape was planned, and they knew where they were heading. It'd have to be fairly random, they end up at some cemetery in Booneville."

Sheriff Cobb nodded, fixing his hat back on his head. "A lot of woods from here to there, but you'd have to know where you're going."

A helicopter flew overhead, and the three looked up.

Charlie had his head tilted back. "Someone oughta let them know they're long gone."

The sheriff said, "I actually think that one is on the lookout for the immigrants, took off from the farm."

Two FBI agents—one male and one female—walked out the front door and headed down the steps from the porch, carrying boxes. Charlie walked toward them and stood at the bottom of the stairs as they came down. "Mind if I ask what you have there?" he said.

"Mostly mail and bills," the female agent said. "The odor's too strong in there."

Charlie reached inside one of the boxes. "You mind?"

The two agents both shook their heads and placed the boxes down on the bottom step.

A state trooper stuck his head out the front door. "We found the interior basement door, covered in paneling."

Charlie nodded, knowing he must've walked past it a couple of times without ever thinking. He was just glad he got down there when he did.

He had a pile of unopened envelopes in his hand, flipping through each one. Most of it looked to be junk mail with little significance. He handed what he had in his hand to the agent and reached in and took some more. "He had all this mail piled up in there?" Charlie said, flipping through the envelopes in his hand.

"It was all already in these two boxes," the male agent said. "You never know what you might find."

Charlie looked up from the envelopes in his hand. "I can think of at least a handful of times I've found a fugitive by looking at the mail they've left behind." He looked toward the house. "No computers of any sort inside?"

Both agents shook their heads. "Nothing."

Charlie tossed the mail in the box, walked past the two agents, and headed inside the house. The odor didn't seem to be as bad as it was earlier. Each room he passed had law enforcement officials inside, whether Kentucky State Police or FBI or investigators from Jackson County Sheriff's Department.

Charlie walked into the kitchen and saw the meat and barrel had been removed and placed somewhere outside. He poked his head out the back door and saw the barrel dumped over, two officers picking through the meat and rotted scraps.

He stepped away and out from the kitchen where the paneling had been ripped from the wall, seeing the door open, but there was no knob. The trim around the door had been removed, so it couldn't have been detected the way the paneling was flat and screwed to the wall around it.

There were plenty of people down in the basement, but Charlie turned from the door and walked into the room with the dining room table and the hutch, with all the silver behind the glass.

There were drawers on the hutch, and Charlie opened each one, not knowing exactly what he might find. In the middle drawer he found a shallow wooden box with "Roberts' Silver and Flatware, Established 1899," etched onto the top.

He took out the wooden box and placed it on the table, opening the lid. The box had a musty smell, and inside it was a set of silverware with twelve forks, made up of two different sizes of six: six knives and twelve spoons also made up of two different sizes. He closed the top and looked at the words etched there.

Kim walked into the room. "What's that?"

Charlie turned from the hutch. "Silverware." He pointed at the silver items behind the glass and turned the box to her so she could read the top. "Looks like what I assume Darnell Roberts' family business either owns—or at one time owned—the company that made, or at least sold the silverware in that box."

Kim lifted the cover and looked inside, closed it again, and took out her phone. She tapped the screen and stared at it for a moment, then looked up at Charlie. "They closed the business over ten years ago."

"Was it around here?"

Kim looked back down at her phone, tapping the screen again with her thumbs. "You're not going to believe it, but the building's in Booneville, listed for lease, with Darnell Roberts shown as the contact, for inquiries."

Charlie and Kim went outside to where Frank had his back to the house, in the middle of talking with six or seven deputies. He turned when Charlie called his name.

"We may have something," Charlie said. "Darnell owns a building out in Booneville, used to manufacture silverware, plates, stuff like that. It's a shot in the dark, but I think we should take a ride out there. It's less than twenty miles; could make it there in fifteen minutes, we hurry up."

"What makes you think they'd stick around?" Frank said. "We were just discussing the possibility they'd likely left the state altogether. Just got word from Sheriff Green a vehicle was reported stolen from a park out by the Southfork Kentucky River. Also reported a motorbike could be heard in the area."

"Then why's everyone standing around?" Charlie said, already heading toward the Suburban. "Deputy Riggins and I are going to take a ride out. You all can hang here and wait, or—"

"Don't be a smart-ass, Charlie," Frank said, following after him. "You think I'm going to let you two go out there by yourselves?" He turned back to the other officials, waving for them to follow. "I'd rather we get enough manpower to surround the place, versus you try and be the hero, if that's all right with you?"

Charlie had already stepped up into the driver's seat of his vehicle, his head hanging out the door. "If you don't think Deputy Riggins and I can handle it, then hop in back," he said.

"You've only got three good legs between the two of you." He opened the back passenger door. "Just hold on a minute, will you?"

"We don't have time to hold on, Frank. I'm sorry. Are you coming or *not*?"

Frank let out a sigh, shaking his head as he climbed into the back seat. "At least let me call Sheriff Green back, let him know. I'm surprised he wouldn't have known Darnell owned a building out there."

Kim turned from the passenger seat as Charlie started the engine and turned the Suburban toward the road. "The business closed over ten years ago, maybe more." She turned her phone to Frank. "Here's the building. No sign or anything other than saying it's for lease. Good chance nobody knows much about it at this point."

Charlie slammed his foot on the gas and hit sixty miles and hour before he even made it all the way out to Conway Road.

Frank strapped the seat belt over himself and dialed his phone. "Sheriff Green, it's Frank Carter. Listen, we're on our way out to Booneville to check out a building my deputy seems to believe could be somewhere the fugitives could be hiding, at least temporarily."

Charlie looked at Frank through the rearview. "We don't want to make a big commotion," he said.

Frank gave him a look, like he needed to shut his mouth and drive. "Maybe about five or six deputies, if they're available." He held the phone away from his ear. "What's the exact address?"

Kim turned in the the passenger seat, looking at her phone as the voice on the GPS told Charlie to turn left onto Kentucky 3630. She said, "One-One-Seven Lone Oak Industrial Park Road."

Frank put the phone up to his ear. "You hear that?" He listened and said to Charlie and Kim, "Sheriff said the vehicle that was reported stolen... was at Owsley County Park, off Route Eleven, not even one minute from that building's address."

"What kind of vehicle was stolen?" Charlie said, looking back at Frank over his right shoulder.

Frank said into the phone, "You have a make and model on that vehicle?" He nodded as he listened, meeting Charlie's eyes in the rearview. "A black 2007 Chevy Impala. Got a rear brake light out."

Charlie said, "Tell him we'll meet him at that same park. Just make sure we've got the name right."

"Owsley County Park," Frank said, then told the sheriff to meet them there in ten minutes. "You don't need to bring a whole army, but we could use a few deputies out on the roads."

Kim looked at her phone and turned to Frank. "We should be there in ten minutes." She opened the glove box and pulled out a tracking device, showing it to Charlie. "Did you know this was in here?"

He nodded. "Yeah, it's from the Morrison case last week. It doesn't work with my phone."

Kim said, "Yeah, because it's already synced with mine." She looked at her phone and clicked the screen. "I thought I left it on his car," she said, then put it back in the glove box.

Charlie's phone rang, and he grabbed it from the center console. He hesitated to answer when he saw it was his ex-wife, Jennie. But although he used to do it all the time when they were married, he chose not to ignore it. "Hello?" he said, acting like he didn't know who was calling.

"I just saw the news," she said. "You found her?"

"We're still looking for the men responsible."

"But you did it, Charlie." She paused. "Is it true she was locked in a meat cooler in the basement?"

Charlie nodded into the phone, half listening, with his eyes on the road, shifting his glance to the speedometer just short of ninety miles per hour. "Hey, do you mind if I call you later? I'm kind of in the middle of something."

She didn't respond right away. "You never give up on anyone, Charlie."

"I just do what I'm supposed to," he said, looking up in the rearview. A Kentucky state trooper was behind him, blue lights spinning. He took the phone from his ear. "We got a trooper, wants to pull me over," he said, looking back at Frank. "I'll call you back, Jennie, when I can."

He hung up and tossed his phone in the center console, glancing in the rearview as he finally slowed down and pulled over to the breakdown lane.

The trooper, who to Charlie looked barely a day over twenty, walked along the side of the Suburban.

"License and—"

Charlie already had his badge out. "Deputy U.S. Marshal Charlie Harlow," he said. "We're in pursuit of two fugitives, on our way out to Booneville."

"U.S. Marshals, huh?" the trooper said, getting a good look at Charlie's badge, almost like he didn't believe him. He looked over at Kim in the passenger seat. "Ma'am?"

Kim showed her badge, and the trooper looked in with a nod.

Frank put down the rear window, holding out *his* badge. "Son, we don't have time for this. Go ahead and call Captain Gorham. We were just with him and about another dozen troopers like yourself in Tyner."

"What's your name, sir?" the young trooper said.

"Chief Deputy Frank Carter."

"Frank Carter?" The trooper glanced in both windows, looking the three over. "I'll be right back," he said, and walked to his vehicle behind them.

"Is he serious?" Frank said, turning in the seat. He stuck his head out the window. "Son?"

But the young trooper didn't look back.

Frank dialed his phone. "This goddamn kid..."

Charlie looked again in the rearview and watched the trooper sit back in the front seat of his cruiser. "I think he *is* serious," Charlie said. "Kid looks barely old enough to be out of high school." He glanced at Frank with the phone to his ear. "Who're you calling?"

"His boss."

He gave Kim a quick glance and shifted into drive. "Well, tell him I'm sorry." Charlie slammed the gas pedal down to the floor and took off, the rear end fishtailing and tires squealing as he cut the wheel into the blaring horns of oncoming traffic.

Chapter 26

Sheriff Marty Green of Owsley County was standing outside his vehicle with three sheriff's vehicles parked next to him at the entrance to Owsley County Park, which was mostly a grass field with a gravel parking lot off Route 11. Six deputies—four men and two women—stood watching Charlie as he drove the Suburban into the lot and stopped next to them.

As he stepped out of the vehicle, along with Frank and Kim, the state trooper who had been following them for the last ten miles drove in right behind them and jumped from his vehicle.

The young trooper was bigger than Charlie had at first noticed, hurrying toward the group.

Charlie braced himself, wondering what the kid was going to do.

The trooper nodded toward the sheriff and said, "Afternoon, Sheriff." He turned to Charlie and stood face-to-face with him. "I don't appreciate you taking off the way you did. I don't care what kind of law enforcement you're a part of. When you're in my state, you should show some respect to your fellow law enforcement officials."

Frank stepped in between them. "All right, son. Why don't you take a deep breath and back up a little. I already spoke with your captain, who assured me we were all on the same page, and you wouldn't be causing any kind of trouble, which I believe right now you are."

The trooper turned to Frank, the young man's eyebrows scrunched over his eyes. "We *are* on the same page. But it doesn't mean I appreciate y'all taking off like that, when I'd asked you to wait while I confirmed a coupla things."

Frank sighed, clearing his throat. "Charlie, would you apologize for taking off the way you did?"

Charlie gave Frank a look, eyebrows raised like he was sure, for a moment, he was making a joke.

But Frank gave him a nod, and Charlie could see in his eyes he wasn't being funny at all.

"We're after two fugitives," Charlie said. "I'm not going to apologize for—"

"Nobody's above the law in Owsley County," the trooper said.

Charlie laughed, realizing maybe the kid may not have been playing with a full deck. "All right. How about I just go ahead and say I apologize. That work for you? So we can move on, worry about these two fugitives before they get any farther ahead of us and disappear for good?" He turned from the trooper and walked with Frank and Kim toward Sheriff Green and his deputies.

The sheriff and the others had grins they looked like they were trying to hide. Sheriff Green leaned into Charlie. "Daniel's a good kid," he said. "I knew his uncle, also with the state police. He was hard up in the same way, although this one's still got some learning to do."

The young trooper walked over to where they all stood. He said, "Captain did say I could offer my assistance, so if there's anything you'd like..."

"Well," Charlie said, "we're looking for a 2007 black Chevy Impala. Got a rear light that's out. We don't know for sure if that's what the fugitives are driving or if they're out there on the road, but right now that's what we've got, and could use some help tracking it down."

Charlie thought maybe the man would leave with that small piece of information, but he stood still, like he was waiting for more.

"You sure you don't need my help apprehending these two fugitives?" he said. "I understand they may be held up inside a building off Lone Oak Industrial Park Road?"

Charlie stared at the young trooper, nodding. "That's right. But we don't want to make too much of a commotion over there. Where we'd really need help"—he looked at the sheriff and his deputies—"is to ensure the two don't slip away again. If it turns out they are inside that building, they're either going to come out shooting or could take off again." He nodded toward Kim. "Go ahead."

Kim had a tablet out with a map of the area around the building. She tapped the screen, then turned it so the others could see. "We'll need at least three vehicles on Lone Oak Industrial Park Road—north, west, and south of the building." She pointed to the screen. "Right here, on Wilson Spur Road, I'd have to say we'll want another three vehicles." She looked up at Sheriff Green. "Perhaps we can get a couple deputies on foot?"

Sheriff Green nodded. "We need more vehicles?" He turned to Frank. "I was under the assumption you had more officials out here."

Frank said to Charlie, "Well, we left a few dozen behind on the farm down in Tyner." He nodded with his chin toward the tall, young trooper. "You want to see if you can get a few more men or women out here to help?" He looked at the tablet Kim was holding. "We could use four vehicles along Route Eleven. If you can't make that happen, I'll call Captain—"

"I'll take care of it, sir." The trooper walked back to his vehicle.

Frank said to the others, "Let's keep in mind they're armed, most likely with automatic weapons." He glanced at the bullet holes in the front of Charlie's Suburban. "We'd like to bring them both in alive, but don't get yourselves killed over it."

Kim said, "We need to keep in mind there's also a fair chance they could already be gone."

Charlie started toward the Suburban. "Let's not waste any more time." He turned. "You all are aware of the Kawasaki motorcycles they took off on? You know that sound of a two-stroke engine, so if you happen to hear something along those lines..."

⸻

Charlie turned the Suburban into the parking lot of the former Roberts' Silver and Flatware building with the lease sign out toward the road and the windows papered over. The building was one level with the brick exterior painted white but the red brick showing through on the edges. Rust stains had formed where water had dripped from the flat roof.

The three stepped out of the vehicle at the same time, guns drawn, Frank turning to Kim as he walked ahead of her. "I thought you were staying in the vehicle." He looked down at the boot she wore on her foot.

"I can handle it," she said.

Charlie stopped, shaking his head. "Frank's right. We need one of us outside anyway." He looked at the building, studying the windows and doors. He left his Glock in the holster and started walking toward a plate-glass side door with kraft paper covering it from the inside.

He looked back at Kim standing still by the Suburban, watching him, then he turned and pulled on the door's handle. He'd assumed it was locked, and sure enough it was.

Frank said, "I'll go around front."

Charlie walked around toward the back of the building, this time removing his Glock. He thought to himself that perhaps his guess, a shot in the dark, was off the mark this time. There were no other vehicles in the parking lot, and no sounds coming from inside the building. He walked toward a loading dock and stood below the concrete steps leading to it, then finally walked up to the dock and tried to raise the steel garage door. It, too, was locked.

He was starting to have his doubts, then noticed a piece of hard mud in front of the door. He bent down and picked it up, looking it over, and right away knew it had dropped off knobby tires. He clicked the two-way on his jacket and whispered into the mic. "Frank, come in back, by the loading dock."

Charlie waited for Frank to respond. "Frank?" He pulled the mic from his vest and looked it over. "Chief? You read me?"

There was no response from Frank.

Charlie started around the building toward the Suburban where Kim had gotten in behind the wheel, the driver's-side window open. He said, "Frank come this way?"

Kim shook her head. "He went around front."

"I know, but…" He pressed the button on the two-way. "Frank?" He started toward the front of the building but turned back to Kim with the Suburban's door open, her good foot down on the ground. "Do me a favor and drive around the other way," he said. "I'll see you on the other side." He continued toward the front of the building and made it to the front door, the glass covered from the inside with paper. Thick and overgrown shrubs to the left and right of the entrance grew across the door.

Charlie pulled the handle and didn't expect it to open. But when it did, he raised his Glock and slowly stepped over the threshold. He kept one foot back to keep the door from closing, letting a streak of light into the darkness in front of him. He held his breath, listening.

He heard a sound behind him and started to turn, but the cold, hard metal of a gun's barrel was pressed up against his skull.

"Good afternoon, Deputy." The person behind him reached around for the Glock and took it from Charlie's hand.

"What'd you do with Frank?" Charlie said.

"He's right in front of you," the man said.

Charlie got a look at the gun: an AK-47.

The man holding it was Steve Crane.

"I oughta shoot you right here," Crane said. "You killed my nephew."

Charlie didn't respond as the door behind him closed and he heard the click of the lock. They stood in darkness, other than the streaks of sunlight that filtered through the paper on the windows.

"Frank?" Charlie said. "You all right?"

The place smelled of grease and mildew.

"Sorry, Charlie," Frank said, his voice clearly strained and quiet. "I'm getting too old for this shit."

Charlie looked ahead into the darkness but could only tell from the direction of Frank's voice that he was somewhere on the floor.

A powerful light turned on and shined straight into Charlie's eyes.

He squinted, lifting his arm up in front of his face to block the light.

The man now facing him—without a doubt, Darnell Roberts—took a step closer to Charlie. "Here's what we're going to do," he said. "First, you're going to go outside and tell that good-looking deputy marshal to back that vehicle up to the loading dock. She tries anything funny, your friend here'll get his body filled with lead.

Once she does that, she'll come in here with us, and what you'll do is help load the back of that Suburban of yours with some items here we need to deliver to an associate of ours."

"Any chance this is the same piece of shit you were planning to sell those women to?" Charlie said.

"That's none of your concern now," the voice said. "But, once you're done loading up the back of that vehicle, what you're going to do is get behind the wheel and drive us out of here, past all those pigs waiting for us."

"Don't do it, Charlie," Frank said.

There was a loud crack, and Frank let out a yelp-like squeal Charlie never imagined he could make.

"Frank?" Charlie said. "You all right?"

All he heard was a moan back from somewhere on the floor.

"Frank?" Charlie tried to take a step forward, but Crane grabbed his shoulder and pushed the barrel harder against his head. "Now, go ahead, use your phone and call her. Tell her what she needs to do." He reached for the mic from the two-way and ripped it from Charlie's vest, then grabbed the transmitter from his belt and smashed it on the floor. "Use your phone."

Charlie squinted with the blinding light coming at him. "Is that light really necessary? I know who you are. You're both wanted men, and no matter what you plan to do with any of us here, you'll never get away."

The light didn't move and Darnell laughed. "I just told you how we're getting away, along with everything we need."

Charlie reached into his pocket and took out his phone. He tapped Kim's number and held it up to his ear. As soon as Kim answered, he said, "Where are you?"

"I'm in back," she said.

"I'm inside," he said. "Got the barrel of a gun pressed into my skull, and Frank's somewhere in front of me on the floor. They want you to back the Suburban up to the loading dock."

"Do you really want me to do that?" she said.

Darnell said, "Put her on speaker."

Charlie paused and said into the phone, "He wants you on speaker." He kept the phone to his ear.

Crane whispered into Charlie's ear, "She calls anyone else for help, Frank's dead. And you'll be next. If that's what she really wants..."

"You hear that?" Charlie said, speaking into the phone.

"I told you to put her on speaker," Darnell snapped.

Charlie tapped the screen. "Okay, you're on speaker."

"What do they want?" Kim said, her voice carrying with a slight echo from the phone.

"They've got something they're trying to deliver."

Darnell yelled, "Just stop with your chit chat and do what I said! Back the goddamn vehicle up to the loading dock and stop stalling."

Charlie said to Kim, "You want to go on and get out of here, I won't hold it against you."

The line went quiet for a moment.

"I'm backing it up now."

"Good girl," Darnell said. "Do anything stupid, you'll have blood on your hands."

Charlie was shoved from behind but stayed on his feet, his arm up in front of his face again to block the bright light.

Finally, the light on the ceiling came on, and Charlie had to squint until his eyes adjusted. He didn't see Darnell anywhere, but Frank was on the floor against a wall ahead of him, blood coming from his mouth. He hurried over and crouched down next to him. "Frank? Frank, can you hear me?"

Frank coughed and lifted his head from the floor. He had a welt on his forehead the size of a golf ball with blood coming down from where he'd apparently been hit.

The building was a wide-open work area with concrete floors and cinder-block walls and twenty-foot-high ceilings. It appeared to be mostly empty, other than a few long work benches. The two Kawasaki bikes were both leaned up against the wall toward the back. Charlie looked at the garage door toward the back, where a dozen or so wooden crates were pushed up against it.

Darnell Roberts walked into the room with an AK-47 strapped over his shoulder. "You're supposed to be a couple of hotshot marshals, from what I hear. But the way you both walked in here, was almost like it's your first day on the job." He laughed.

Charlie nodded toward the crates. "What's in those?"

"Guns," he said. "I like to diversify my businesses. Crops, guns, and bitches; it's where the money's at."

Charlie stood up and helped Frank to his feet. "If you think I'm going to somehow help you move illegal weapons, you've got another think comin'." He turned to Crane, standing by the door with the same automatic weapon Darnell had strapped over his back. Charlie said,

"Haley trusted you. But you're nothing but a lowlife piece of shit."

Steve Crane grinned. "Every man's entitled to his opinion," he said. "She was well taken care of."

"Locked in a cooler in the basement? Then, what? You were going to sell her and the others, like she's some kind of goddamn livestock?"

From the other side of the room, Darnell said, "Well, she certainly was a fine piece of meat."

Charlie didn't pause or even think for a second and charged at Darnell Roberts, empty handed and not sure what he was going to do, but Darnell raised the AK-47 at him.

Charlie didn't stop. He kept going at him, like he dared Darnell to pull the trigger. And just when he got close enough, Darnell Roberts didn't pull the trigger, but turned his weapon and hit Charlie square in the head with the buttstock, sending him with a stumble backward.

Charlie felt the warmth of his own blood drip down his face but got his footing and went back at Darnell.

As he took the next step, the rapid fire from behind him went off.

Charlie stopped and ducked, his hands over his head, and glanced back at Crane, the gun pointed at Charlie.

"Move another inch, I'll take your legs right out from under you," Crane said.

Charlie had to use the sleeve of his jacket to wipe the blood from his face. He glanced at Frank looking too weak to move. They'd beaten him pretty good.

"Darnell pulled the kraft paper aside and peeked out the window, then walked to the garage door and lifted it open. The sunlight poured inside.

Charlie looked out at the Suburban parked with the rear end to the loading dock. He could see Kim facing the other way waiting in the front seat.

"Let her go," Charlie said. "You don't need her."

Darnell Roberts stepped to the edge of the loading dock and held his AK-47 pointed toward the Suburban, slowly stepping down the steps to ground level. He yelled to Kim, "I hope you were smart enough you didn't alert your friends out there!" He slowly walked toward the passenger side.

Charlie glanced at Frank, who had sat back down on the floor, and started toward the opening.

"Where you think you're going?" Crane said, walking up behind Charlie.

Charlie wasn't armed and for the most part knew he was useless. He stopped and looked over his shoulder at Crane.

A shot fired from outside, and Charlie saw Darnell Roberts drop to the ground. Another shot fired, with Kim sliding over from the driver's seat to the passenger side where she stepped out, holding her gun on Darnell.

Crane raced from inside the building toward the loading dock, past Charlie, his gun pointed toward Kim.

But Charlie stepped in his way and drove his shoulder into him, knocking him to the ground.

Steve Crane fell off the dock and dropped down to the asphalt, but he hadn't dropped his gun and came up firing before Kim or Charlie could do a thing.

"Kim!" Charlie yelled, watching her as she ran around the corner of the building for cover, firing behind her toward Darnell and Crane before she disappeared.

She exchanged fire with the two men, the shots lasting for another three or four minutes until they stopped.

Although Darnell was bleeding from just above his chest, with blood soaking through his shirt, he was up on his feet.

Charlie wondered if Kim had been hit, or if she got out of there. Her gun, a Glock like Charlie's, was no match for two AK-47s.

Darnell Roberts pointed his gun at Charlie. "Load those goddamn crates in the back of that vehicle." He looked at his buddy, Crane. "Where the hell'd that pretty deputy run off to? Go see if maybe we got her." He coughed into his hand, then looked at it.

Charlie thought maybe he could turn and run, go right out the front door. But Frank didn't look to be in any condition to move. And he wasn't about to leave him behind.

Darnell had the gun pointed at him. "Get your ass moving."

Crane came around the corner, shaking his head. "I don't know where she is. She's gone."

Darnell looked around from where he stood, then up at Charlie. "Maybe she decided to leave you and the old man hanging?" He laughed. "Too bad. She's a little old, but I bet she could've turned me a little bit of pocket money with one of my clients." His laugh was followed by a cough, and once again he looked into his hand.

Charlie could see the blood. "This isn't going to work," he said. "We have law enforcement officials all over the area. You won't make it half a mile."

Darnell Roberts wiped his mouth with the back of his hand. "Well, I'm hoping with you behind the wheel, we won't have as much to worry about."

Chapter 27

D ARNELL R OBERTS SAT IN the passenger seat next to Charlie, blood coming through his shirt and his face pale white. He slouched down in the seat and held a pistol on Charlie in the driver's seat, behind the wheel, as they drove slowly past the two deputies on foot, in the breakdown lane off Kentucky 11.

The two deputies watched, staring into the Suburban, but had already been informed by Charlie they'd have to stand down.

The roadblocks were called off and cleared.

Charlie looked in the rearview mirror at Frank in the back seat, with Steve Crane next to him holding the AK-47, pointed at him.

Frank looked like he might've been feeling a little better, some color back in his face, but his voice still wasn't the same when he spoke up. He cleared his throat before he spoke. "Even if you kill us, you think every law enforcement official this side of Missouri doesn't know what's going on? That you're in this vehicle?"

Darnell was turned in the seat, facing Charlie, and looked back toward Frank. "If they want the blood of two U.S. Marshals on their hands, then maybe they'll just go ahead and see if they'd like to give it a try and stop us. But, I don't know... I'd say I'm feeling pretty good about how things are going right now." He shifted his gaze to Crane. "At least, it's looking better than it did earlier, before these two walked right in as if we weren't gonna be waiting for 'em." He laughed and once again followed it with a long, deep cough.

Charlie didn't think the man looked too good at all, wondering if the bullet Kim had hit him with did more damage than Darnell Roberts wanted to believe. Charlie said to him, "So, when are you going to tell me exactly where we're going?"

"You'll know when we get there." He leaned toward Charlie and took a look at the gauges on the dashboard. "You ain't got much gas in this thing." He looked again at the dash. "What's that, not even half a tank?" He shifted in the seat, the gun in his hand resting on his thigh but still pointed at Charlie. "What's this vehicle get: ten, fifteen to the gallon?"

Charlie glanced at him, annoyed, like the guy wanted to have some kind of casual conversation. "No idea," he said, even though he knew exactly what it got. He didn't like driving the big gas guzzler, but he got it cheap before it went to auction. "You tell me where we're going, I'll tell you if we're gonna make it."

Darnell stared at Charlie, his eyes narrowed like he was thinking it through.

"Otherwise, we gotta stop for gas, I can't promise you what might happen."

"We got about two hours ahead of us," Darnell said, pointing toward the road. "Stay here on Eleven, head south for about another twenty-five miles, till you get to Four-Twenty-One."

Charlie didn't respond, figured he'd do everything the man asked, the way the gun was pointed at him. He was going to be patient, something he wasn't always capable of but knew it'd be his only choice, not to mention having a chance these two were going to lead him to the bigger fish.

———

They'd been on the road for a little over an hour and a half, Darnell Roberts in the passenger seat breathing heavy, looking worse than he did when they left, the way his blood had soaked through his shirt. He let out a deep cough every mile or so, and had Charlie turn off the air-conditioning because he was cold.

"This man needs to get to the hospital," Frank said, looking up at Charlie from the back seat.

Charlie nodded but knew Darnell wasn't going to go for it. "If you don't want to stop because you're afraid you're going to miss out on whatever money you're supposed to be getting for these guns, I'm not sure it'll make much of a difference if you're dead when we get to wherever it is we're going."

Darnell lifted the gun from his thigh, giving the muzzle a slight wiggle, pointing it toward Charlie. "Just shut up and drive until I tell you not to."

"Well," Charlie said. "That's another problem we may have." He nodded toward the dashboard in front of him. "We're about ready to be driving on fumes. So unless we're about to be wherever it is we're going, I'd suggest we pull off and get us some gas." He glanced up in the rearview at Frank, scratching the back of his neck as he turned to look at Darnell. "There's a station up about another mile from here. Probably the last one before we get to the Tennessee line."

"How do you know there's a gas station?" Crane said from the back.

Charlie said, "You think this is the first time I've been in a car with a fugitive up here in Kentucky? I've covered more of these roads and highways than I care to think about.”

Crane just stared back at him, not saying much else.

“So, what’s it going to be?” Charlie said. “You want to carry these the rest of the way? Or are we going to pull off and get some gas.”

Darnell Roberts coughed into his hand, looking back at Crane. “You get out and pump,” he said. “I’ll keep an eye on these two.” He held out his hands and looked down at his shirt. “I can’t let anyone see me like this.”

Charlie eyeballed the gun in Darnell’s hand, noticing the way he was getting more careless with it, the way he was holding it, his wrist a lot looser with it now.

“Don’t get any ideas,” Darnell said, looking right into Charlie’s eyes like he knew what Charlie was thinking.

“They’re usually not very good anyway,” he said.

“Huh?”

“My ideas. They’re never very good.” He gave Darnell a look out of the corner of his eye and grinned. “Like walking into that building, not realizing Crane must’ve been hiding in those shrubs.” He shook his head, his lips pressed together. “Nope, not a very good idea.”

Darnell just stared back at him. “You should’ve just stayed out of it when you had the chance.”

Charlie had his eyes on the road. “But, I wouldn’t be doing my job if I did.” He again looked at Darnell. “Isn’t that what all this is about? We're all just doing our jobs? I mean, I look for the bad guys—like you—and then, well, Crane back there cleans out the fountain at the shopping center." He looked at Crane in the back. "Now, you mind telling me something? Is the whole reason you worked there so you can get your hands on women and sell them like livestock? Or is this just something part-time you decided to jump into?"

Crane looked confused, like he couldn't tell if Charlie was playing with him or if he was asking a serious question.

"Me and Darnell go back a long ways."

"So, what you're saying is Haley wasn't the first?" He looked ahead at the road but shifted his eyes back to the rearview. "What about that young woman your nephew took out to Mount Mitchell, left her body in the woods? What happened there? For some reason, one of you decided you'd rather kill her?"

"You don't have to tell him nothing," Darnell said, looking back at Crane.

But Crane ignored him. "We didn't kill her. She was hurt when Travis tried to get her in the back of his truck. She hit her head, died right there. He'd never kill anyone. Travis was a good kid."

Charlie and Frank both laughed. "A good kid, huh?"

"Don't think I'm going to forget what you did to him," Crane said, shifting his grip on the AK-47 he kept pointed at Frank.

"So, if you're planning to kill me, then I guess I might have nothing to lose at this point?"

Darnell said. "You think we're just going to let you go when all's said and done?" He laughed, then coughed for a good minute before he finally stopped.

Charlie looked at the fuel gauge and was almost certain they were going to run out of gas. The station he knew of was coming up ahead, right after the treatment plant he remembered up on the right, off Route 25, in Pineville. "This is our last shot at putting some fuel in the tank," he said. "We don't stop now, we're not going to make it another five miles."

"I don't see where it is," Darnell said.

Charlie nodded toward the turn up ahead. "Down that road to the right." He looked at Darnell closing his eyes, wondering if the man might be dying right there before they got much farther.

But Darnell's eyes sprang open, and he straightened up in the seat, coughing. He turned to Crane. "You have money?"

Crane shook his head. "Maybe a few dollars on a credit card, but—"

"You want me to get out and pump?" Charlie said. "I don't mind paying…"

"Shut up," Darnell said, raising the gun to him. "I told you, you're staying right where you are."

"Actually, I really gotta pee," Charlie said. "So if we can just pull over at some point?"

Darnell shook his head. "I don't care if you pee your pants right here. It's your car."

Frank said, "You two boys, there's no police anywhere around us at this point. What's the sense in you keeping us here anymore? You've done it. You gotten away."

Charlie looked in the mirror at Frank, wondering why he'd even bother asking.

"You think we're just going to let you two go?" Darnell said, looking into the back at Frank. "No chance, old man. I can just see it now: we let you out, twenty-five deputies are up our asses."

Charlie said, "Nobody's following. You heard me tell them on the phone not to follow, and they won't take a chance, with two law enforcement officials' lives at stake."

"Killing us isn't gonna do you much good, is it?" Frank said, looking out the window with the gas station coming up on the right. "You get your gas, leave us right there, and go on your way. I don't see what harm it'd do."

"You can keep the vehicle," Charlie said. "Been thinking about getting something better on gas, anyhow."

Darnell stared at Charlie, then turned, looking back at Crane like he was thinking it over.

Charlie turned into the Sunoco gas station and stopped next to one of four pumps. He wasn't even sure, by the looks of the old pumps, whether they even took credit cards, and one of them would have to go inside and pay. He turned off the engine. "She runs better with the good stuff, if you don't mind."

Darnell held out his hand, dried blood covering it, toward Charlie. "Give me a credit card?"

"Me?" Charlie said, a crooked grin on his face. "You want me to pay for the gas?"

"It's your vehicle."

Charlie looked him over, the way his face was whiter than it was before, still bleeding through the shirt but not like it was an hour earlier. "You really oughta get that looked at," he said. "Or you're not gonna make it wherever we're going." He leaned forward and pulled out his wallet, took a credit card out, and handed it to Darnell.

Darnell took it and gave it to Crane. "Fill it up."

Crane handed the AK-47 to Darnell and stepped out of the Suburban. He stood in front of the pump for a moment, then knocked on the passenger-side window.

Darnell put it down and Crane said. "This pump doesn't take credit cards."

"Then go inside," Darnell said.

Crane nodded toward Charlie. "It's got his name on the card."

"That's all right," Charlie said. "They don't even check anymore."

"He's right," Darnell said. "Now, hurry up. We're gonna be late."

Chapter 28

Charlie turned the wheel when Darnell told him to and drove down a long dirt road that cut between thick woods, with large trees hanging overhead. They continued for at least the length of a football field, stopping before a wide building with a blue steel exterior. The sign over the front door said, Carmen's Sausage Factory. There were trucks parked around the side of the building and an older, green-panel truck parked in front. A white Mercedes with dark-tinted windows was parked next to it.

Darnell was leaning back against the passenger door, hadn't taken the gun off Charlie, but the way his body appeared limp, his shoulders slouched, made Charlie wonder if the man was going to live.

"Get out," he said, his voice quiet and weak. "Give me the keys."

Charlie pulled his keys from the ignition and handed them to Darnell, then stepped out of the Suburban.

Frank got out from the back with Steve Crane sliding out after him, holding the AK-47 on him. The two walked around the Suburban to where Charlie stood, just outside the driver's-side door, with Crane holding the gun on both of them.

Charlie turned his ear, hearing a loud buzzing sound coming from somewhere out toward the road or in the woods. At first, he thought it might've been a chainsaw.

But then the sound quieted until it stopped altogether. Charlie wondered who else heard it, or if they'd even paid enough attention.

"Keep an eye on them," Darnell said, walking toward the building with his hand pressed against his chest. But before he got to the door, a man with white hair but dark and leatherlike skin, walked outside to greet him.

The man's eyes opened wide, looking Darnell over. With a Spanish accent, the man said, "What happened? You are bleeding."

Darnell looked down at himself, nodding. "I got shot."

The man glanced over at Charlie and Frank. "Who are the Gringos?"

Darnell cleared his throat. "Well, don't be alarmed," he said. "They are actually, uh... They're U.S. Marshals."

The man's eyes almost bugged out of his head. He stared at Frank and Charlie, quiet as he seemed to be processing what exactly could have been going on. His voice raised, he said to Darnell, "Have you lost your mind?"

Darnell shook his head. "I had no choice. They had us surrounded, and these two... they were our only way out."

"Your only way out? I don't understand? But, why would you bring them here? What are you planning to do with them?"

Darnell shrugged, giving Charlie and Frank a quick look. "Kill them."

The man stared at Charlie, looking him over, then turned to Frank before he walked toward them and peeked inside the Suburban. The driver's-side door was still open as he leaned in, then walked around to the rear and opened the liftgate. He stepped out from behind it. "Where are they?"

"They're in the crates," Darnell said, followed by a cough.

The man shook his head. "You know what I'm talking about. I see the crates back here. The girls."

"Well," Darnell said, slowly walking toward him. "We had a little problem, back at my farm."

The man cocked his head back, his eyebrows tight over his eyes, staring back at Darnell.

Darnell nodded toward Charlie. "This man has caused us problems."

The man held his gaze on Darnell and didn't move a muscle for a least thirty seconds, staring back at him like he could burn Darnell's face with his eyes. "You do not have the girls?"

Darnell nodded, coughing. "I'm sorry. There was nothing we could do."

"You did not call me to tell me this? You think, bringing me these guns, is going to make up for the fact you—"

"It's thirty thousand dollars' worth," Crane said.

The man turned his gaze to him. "Did I ask you to speak?"

Steve Crane shook his head. "No, sir."

Two more men came out from inside the building and walked to the rear of the Suburban, reached in, and each grabbed a crate. They went back inside the building, came out and took two more crates, continuing until they had removed everything from the vehicle.

When they were done unloading, the white-haired man grabbed one of the two by the arm and whispered into his ear.

The man nodded, turned, and stepped toward Darnell, taking him by the arm. The other went into the building and came back out with an automatic weapon, walking ahead of them around the side of the building as the man with Darnell followed.

"What are you doing?" Darnell said, looking at the white-haired man as the other dragged him around the side.

"You have made a mistake, Roberts," the man said, shaking his head. He looked at Crane. "I am going to let you live for now." He looked at Charlie and Frank. "But I don't see the need for these two any longer. I would like you to kill them, but I don't want it done here."

"What about Darnell?" Crane said, a worried look on his face.

But Darnell was already gone, somewhere around the back of the building.

The quiet around was interrupted by the brief sound of an automatic weapon; rapid gunfire rang out. Birds flew from trees and screeched, but then the sounds were gone, the quiet back.

Charlie could see the two men dragging Darnell's body away from the building in the opposite direction, toward another smaller building before the woods.

"So what kind of operation you have going here?" Charlie said. "Human trafficking? Gun trafficking? What else?" He looked around the property. "I'd have to guess you at least have some dealing with drugs, no?

Heroin? Although I'd have to guess kidnapping young women has the highest margin, no?"

Frank said, "Charlie," as if he didn't want him to say another word and stir up any more trouble than they were already in.

The white-haired man shrugged, looking Charlie up and down. "I know all about you... the U.S. Marshals Service. You are like a cowboy." He looked around and laughed. "Where is your horse?"

Charlie shook his head. "I'm not a cowboy. And I don't really like horses that much. I mean, I like them from afar, but they make me nervous, being as strong as they are." He nodded toward the Suburban. "Although, with gas prices the way they are, I've been thinking of some kind of alternative to this gas guzzler, so..."

Frank shook his head. "Jesus, Charlie."

The man laughed, nodding as he wagged a finger at Charlie. "You are a funny one." But the smile left his face, and he nodded at Crane. "Go ahead, shoot them."

The buzzing sound Charlie heard earlier had started up again, but this time it was louder and closer, and he wasn't the only one who could hear it.

The white-haired man looked down the dirt road.

Charlie realized it was a two-stroke engine, and it was coming toward them, although he couldn't tell from where.

The white-haired man yelled out something in Spanish, and the two men who were off in the distance left Darnell's body on the ground and started to run back toward the building.

The winding, screaming sound grew louder, and the sound of an automatic weapon rang out from somewhere behind the building.

Charlie looked and watched the two men who had dragged Robert's body collapse into the tall grass as the motorbike came around the corner behind the building, the engine whining.

The rider wore a black helmet and dark face shield, holding a rifle, but turned around toward the back of the building.

The man with the white hair ran inside.

Charlie looked at Steve Crane with the confusion on his face looking toward wherever the bike had gone.

But Charlie grabbed the barrel of Crane's gun and turned it up, throwing his knee into Crane's crotch and flipping him over his back to the ground. He ripped the AK-47 from Crane's hands and pointed it down at him. "Don't move, you piece of shit."

Frank reached down and removed the Glock from the back of Crane's pants and held it up for Charlie. "This one yours?"

Charlie nodded, handing Frank the AK-47 and taking back his Glock. He dragged Steve Crane by his shirt toward the back of the Suburban, reaching inside for a spare set of handcuffs. He clipped one end on Crane's wrist, the other to the steel under the rear bumper, leaving him on the ground.

Frank and Charlie stayed and took cover behind the Suburban, looking toward the side of the building.

"Who the hell is it?" Frank said.

Charlie didn't answer, poking his head out the side. "Someone with us, I hope," he said, then caught a glimpse of the person from the bike walking around the corner of the building, removing the helmet.

He looked down and saw the boot. "Are you kidding me?" Charlie said, turning to Frank. "It's Deputy Riggins."

Kim looked at Charlie, hurrying toward them, and the three stood behind the Suburban. She glanced down at Steve Crane. "Where's the other one?"

"Dead," Frank said. "Not far from where you took out the other two."

Charlie had his head poked out, looking at the front door of the building. "Let's go get him," he said, then took off toward the door with his Glock in his hand but by his side.

Kim and Frank both followed.

Charlie stood to the side of the door waiting for the two.

Kim was next to him, to the right of the door.

Charlie said to her, "You rode that bike the whole way down here?"

"I guess nobody noticed I'd turned on the tracker?"

"The one in the glove box?" Charlie said.

Kim nodded. "Tried to stay with you, but rode in the woods for most of the ride, except for the two times I had to stop for gas. Those bikes are not made for long-distance riding."

"I didn't know you knew how to ride," Frank said, his voice low as Charlie yanked on the front door, gun raised.

"You ready?" Charlie said.

Kim whispered to Frank, "I had a Yamaha YZ-125, growing up."

"Someone want to go around back?" Charlie said.

Frank nodded and took off with the AK-47 in his hands.

Kim followed after Charlie, and the two went inside.

On the left, just inside the door, was a reception desk behind glass but the chair wasn't occupied. There was a hallway straight ahead with a door on the end, the same blue steel walls inside as were used on the exterior. Charlie opened the door into what looked like a manufacturing floor with machines and equipment, not knowing which machine was used for what. He didn't know much about how sausage was made.

They continued across the area toward an exterior door. Charlie pushed it open, and Frank was standing outside, pointing the AK-47 right at him.

"Jesus, Charlie. I almost shot you right in the—"

"Where the hell'd he go?" Charlie said, stepping outside looking back and forth. He turned when he heard a car's engine, tucked his gun in his pants and ran toward the motorbike Kim had parked toward the corner of the building. He jumped on top of it, kicked the starter, and took off, the rear tire spinning as he leaned, turning the corner.

The white Mercedes that was parked out front was driving fast, away from him on the dirt road.

Charlie turned his wrist and gave it as much gas as it would take, lifting the front wheel off the ground, although not on purpose. The Kawasaki's engine screamed as Charlie went after the Mercedes.

He caught up in no time at all, riding behind the car, then cutting around to the side of it. He pulled up next to the driver's side and took his Glock out from the back of his pants.

He could barely see the driver inside the car through the dark-tinted windows but saw enough to know it was the white-haired man. Charlie pointed the gun toward the window, but the driver yanked the wheel and knocked Charlie off his path on the narrowing road.

The bike almost tipped, swerving, as Charlie maintained control with the Mercedes speeding ahead of him. But Charlie had kept the Glock in his hand, raised it, and fired at the rear wheel. With one shot, he hit the tire. He rolled his wrist and gave the Kawasaki more gas, raising the Glock again and firing another shot, this time hitting the front left tire.

The Mercedes swerved as it cut off the road out of control and crashed into a large red maple halfway into the woods.

Charlie jumped off the bike as he dumped it and ran toward the car. The man started to open the door, but Charlie was already there and yanked the door open, ripping the man from the driver's seat and tossing him to the ground, then sticking the Glock inches from his face. "Make one move, I'll pull this trigger. And believe me when I tell you, part of me's hoping you have a twitch."

Charlie looked down the road at police vehicles coming toward him, blue lights spinning. The first car there was from the Buncombe County Sheriff's Office, with Sheriff Cobb behind the wheel. Another dozen cars had arrived, law enforcement officials from three different counties, one behind the other.

The sheriff stepped out of the car and walked toward Charlie with his gun in his hand. "Looks like you got everything under control?"

Charlie didn't respond, just said, "You mind I borrow your handcuffs?"

Chapter 29

CHARLIE THREW BACK HIS second shot of Jack Daniels and turned to look at the bruise on Frank's head. He raised his hand to Lindsey and gestured for her to pour them two more.

Frank said, "You know, Sheriff Cobb told me after his next term, you should think about running for sheriff."

Charlie laughed. "Was he serious?"

Frank shook his head. "That's what I asked him. I'd like to think he was kidding, otherwise I'm not so sure I trust his judgment the way I used to." He sipped his drink and placed the glass down. "I gotta hit the head." He got up from the stool and nodded toward his drink. "That's my last one. I'm serious this time. This old man needs some rest."

Charlie grinned, watching Frank walk along the bar toward the restroom, each step with a more pronounced limp than the last time they were at the Coyote Grille.

Lindsey stepped over and leaned with her elbows down, looking into Charlie's eyes from the other side of the bar. "I missed you," she said. "I hope you're going to hang around tonight? I could use some company after I lock up." She bit her lower lip and smiled, reaching for Charlie's hand.

Charlie sipped his Jack Daniels and didn't exactly answer. He was tired, but he didn't think it'd be right to tell her that.

Frank walked out of the restroom toward them, and Lindsey straightened up off the bar, wiping her hands with the towel draped over her shoulder.

Frank had the phone up to his ear, nodding. "Well, I hate to hear that, but I am going to put my foot down this time. I don't even want to see your face in that office for a minute." He nodded, listening, as he sat back down on the stool. "You take care of yourself. We'll check in on you tomorrow." He tapped the screen and set the phone on the bar.

"Everything all right?" Charlie said.

Frank picked up his glass, nodding. "Well, Deputy Riggins really mangled up her leg this time. She's going to be set back three more weeks, at least. Out of work that whole time."

"I'd say it was worth it," Charlie said.

"Worth it?" Frank gave Charlie a quick look. "I'm without my best deputy for three weeks, and—"

Charlie laughed. "Are you trying to tell me something?"

Frank shook his head. "No."

Charlie said, "So, then, what am *I*? Second best?"

Frank didn't respond. His phone buzzed and he lifted it, looking at the screen. "Oh, well, looks like we got ourselves a lead."

"What's that?"

"James Keegan and his sister may have been spotted inside a Waffle House just outside Jacksonville, across from a Holiday Inn they may be staying at."

Charlie knew what was coming next but was afraid to ask. He looked over at Lindsey and watched her serve a couple of truck drivers down the far end of the bar. He threw back his Jack Daniels.

Frank said, "How do you feel about heading down there in the morning?"

Charlie shrugged, nodding, but didn't say much else. It was just how the job went, one case to the next. He'd thought about trying to go visit Haley and her dad, see how they were doing. But maybe it could wait. He was just happy she was all right, back living somewhere with a roof over her head.

Frank finished his drink and got up from the stool. He grabbed his jacket off the rack to the right of the door. "Coldest night in a while," he said.

Charlie said, "Good night for sleeping."

Frank stood at the door, looking from Charlie to Lindsey as he cracked a slight smile. "Make sure you get some rest, Charlie." He walked out the door and closed it behind him.

"Good night, Frank," Lindsey said, after he'd already left, walking over to Charlie. "You want another one?"

He looked into his empty glass and thought about it for a moment. "I think I'd better not."

Lindsey opened her mouth to speak but Charlie's phone rang. He looked at the screen and saw it was Jennie. "Sorry, Lindsey, let me just step outside and grab this. It's work." He got up from the stool and walked out into the cold air outside on the deck. He left his jacket hanging on the hook inside and felt a chill as he put the phone up to his ear. "Hey..."

"Where are you?" she said.

"I thought once the divorce was final you'd stop asking me questions like that?"

"I can't ask you where you are anymore?"

Charlie let out a small laugh, leaning on the railing. He looked down over the parking lot, seeing the taillights on Frank's truck driving away. "I was meeting with Frank."

"Are you all right?" she said. "You told me you'd call me back, but—"

"I'm sorry. I was going to. But, I don't know, Jennie. I don't get any of the benefits of being married, but still got you checking in on me all the time. Maybe we need to break that habit somehow. It'll be good for you, don't you think?"

The line went quiet. "Sorry," she said. "I was worried."

"I know. But that's the problem. You wanted a divorce so you didn't have to worry all the time. But I'm not sure it's accomplished much of what it was supposed to."

He waited for a response, but there wasn't one. Not right away.

"Jennie?"

"Yeah?"

He turned and looked toward the front door of the bar as the last two customers walked out. Lindsey was right behind them inside and flipped the sign on the window to CLOSED. He looked at his watch as the bright Coyote Grille sign over the door went dark.

He said into the phone, "Can I call you tomorrow? I'll catch you up on everything that went down."

"I saw on the news there were ten more women locked down there."

"Seven women and three young males. This was a serious operation, but there's plenty more of it going on out there, bigger than this."

"And they would've never gotten there if it weren't for you," Jennie said. "I hope they realize that."

"I don't worry about that, Jennie. You know I don't."

"I know," she said. "I'm just saying, if you'd given up the way some people wanted you to…"

Charlie nodded, looking down at the Suburban parked under the only light in the parking lot. "I gotta head out in the morning, down to Jacksonville."

"Are you serious?" she said.

"Why wouldn't I be? You know how it works."

The phone went quiet.

"Everything all right with you?" Charlie said, trying to change the topic away from his work.

"The front stairs look nice," she said. "I thought maybe you'd want to come down and see how they came out."

Charlie looked through the window into the bar at Lindsey holding a broom, sweeping the floor. "How about I give you a call on my way down to Jacksonville? I'll be in the car for five or six hours tomorrow."

"Not tonight?" she said.

Charlie swallowed. "Tonight? It's kind of late, isn't it?" He looked in at Lindsey, then turned back to the parking lot. "Jennie? You want to tell me what's going on with you?"

The line went quiet.

"Jennie?"

"I'm sorry," she said. "You're right. It's late. I just thought... I didn't know if maybe you wanted to talk, or..."

He ran his hand through his hair, his mouth so dry he knew he'd need that drink he'd just turned down. "I don't know what you're doing here, Jennie. The way you've been acting lately, I'm starting to think you like me more now than when we were married."

There was more silence.

"I'm sorry," she said. "You're right. I... I had a couple glasses of wine, and... Forget I said anything. Just call me tomorrow, Charlie. Good night."

"Jennie?"

She didn't respond. He looked at his phone and saw she'd hung up.

Lindsey opened the door and poked her head out. "Temperature really dropped out here," she said. "You coming in? So I can lock this door?"

Charlie glanced one more time at his phone, slipped it into his pocket, and walked toward the door Lindsey held open for him. When he got close enough, she grabbed him by the shirt and smacked him on the lips with a wet kiss, wrapping her arms around his neck as she pulled him closer.

His phone rang in his pocket, but he didn't answer it. He reached his hand in, felt for the button and turned it off.

JAKE HORN MYSTERIES
Murder at Morrissey Motel
Body on the Beach

CRIME FICTION/STANDALONES
Biscayne Boogie
Tell Them I'm Dead
Drag the Man Down
Half Cocked
Danny Womack's .38

Join the email newsletter!

Be the first to know about my new releases, subscriber-only sales, and author news and updates. Visit **GregoryPayette.com** to join.